Joshua was deepening his kiss, urging her lips apart, and when he felt a faint response his arms tightened. He hadn't lost her! She might believe that she hated him, but her body was telling a different story.

She suddenly jerked free. "Get away from me!" she yelled, her eyes feverishly bright. "Don't ever do that again or I'll make sure you regret it for the rest of your life."

"You could have stopped me any time you liked," he said smartly. "But you didn't. Why was that, I wonder? Were you enjoying it? Was it only belatedly that you remembered who you were kissing? It was good for us once—why not again?"

"Because I'm not the same person," she retorted. "You threw me out, don't forget. If I have to work and live with you, then so be it, but as for anything else—it's out of the question."

"I think you enjoyed my kiss," he said calmly. "You're simply afraid to admit it, even to yourself."

Born in the industrial heart of England, **MARGARET MAYO** now lives in a Staffordshire countryside village. She became a writer by accident, after attempting to write a short story when she was almost forty, and now writing is one of the most enjoyable parts of her life. She combines her hobby of photography with her research.

Margaret Mayo

RECLAIMING HIS BRIDE

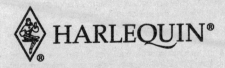

HARLEQUIN®

TORONTO • NEW YORK • LONDON
AMSTERDAM • PARIS • SYDNEY • HAMBURG
STOCKHOLM • ATHENS • TOKYO • MILAN • MADRID
PRAGUE • WARSAW • BUDAPEST • AUCKLAND

ISBN 0-373-18831-5

RECLAIMING HIS BRIDE

First North American Publication 2004.

Copyright © 2004 by Margaret Mayo.

This edition published by arrangement with Harlequin Books S.A.

® and TM are trademarks of the publisher. Trademarks indicated with ® are registered in the United States Patent and Trademark Office, the Canadian Trade Marks Office and in other countries.

www.eHarlequin.com

Printed in U.S.A.

CHAPTER ONE

'IT WAS a good ploy, leaving the vineyard to us.' Joshua's eyes roved slowly over the acres of vines which stretched out in front of them. Their orderly rows ran halfway across the valley, meeting the eucalyptus and scrub, and the sky above was an incredibly hot blue. It might have been a pleasure tackling this new venture in a country the other side of the world, except that it wasn't. It was out of the question. Totally.

Leanne tossed her head, blonde hair flying, wide green eyes flashing her irritation. 'It was no ploy. They were simply being fair.'

Joshua didn't think so. He was under no delusion that Leanne's mother and his father had wanted more than anything in the world for them to reconcile their differences. It had devastated them both when their offspring divorced and they never lost an opportunity to suggest that they had been a bit premature.

Personally he didn't think so. He had given Leanne every chance and she had repaid him by going to bed with his brother. 'We both know that they hoped we would one day get back together,' he responded tersely. 'But it can never be.'

'I agree.' She glared hostilely into his sapphire-blue eyes. 'When are you returning to England?'

Joshua saw little of the sweet young girl who had once been his wife, the girl who had been so full of fun and laughter. Her face was pale and tightly drawn, her eyes full of resentment. 'I think the sooner the better.' But there were things to be dealt with. The major one being to get rid of his share of the vineyard; Leanne could have the lot as far as he was concerned.

He couldn't help thinking back to the day they had met. Leanne's father had died and she had come to England with her mother to stay with relatives for a while. He had met her at a party when she was just seventeen. He had fallen instantly in love, the eight-year age gap not mattering in the least. He had been enchanted by this young Australian girl with the mass of blonde hair and laughing green eyes. She was so easy to get on with that they'd known everything about each other in no time at all.

'Will you marry me?' Joshua held Leanne's hands tightly and his eyes never left hers. For ten months he had known this girl and simply looking at her sent his testosterone levels sky-high. But he didn't want physical emotions persuading her at this moment. He wanted her to agree to be his wife for all the right reasons, and it seemed like an eternity before she gave him her answer.

It was more a breathless whisper than actual words and he had to bend his head low to hear. 'Yes, Joshua. Yes, I will. I love you.'

'And I love you too, my dearest darling. Nothing or no one will ever part us. Marriage is a lifetime commitment. Do you agree?'

She nodded and lifted her mouth for his kiss. 'I will never want anyone else for as long as I live. Never.'

*   *   *

Leanne's mother, Pauline, was equally happy. When Leanne told her about Joshua's proposal she hugged her tightly. 'He's a good man, Leanne, you'll never find anyone better.'

'I know, Mum, I know.'

And when Pauline met Joshua's father and eventually fell in love with him too it seemed as though the black hole left behind by her father's death was finally healing. 'Let's have a double wedding?' Leanne suggested excitedly.

'Darling, I couldn't,' said her mother at once. 'I can't spoil your special day; it would be unfair.'

'No, Mum,' said Leanne, shaking her head. 'It would make it even more special. Please say yes.'

And so the two marriages took place, and afterwards her new stepfather returned to Australia with her mother to help run the vineyard that had been sadly neglected.

Joshua took charge of the family consultancy business, together with his younger brother, Mark, and Leanne was completely happy living in London. Coming from the wide-open spaces of South Australia, she had at first found it strange and constrictive, but in no time she'd come to terms with it and grew to love exploring all its lesser-known places.

But then had come the dark days when Joshua lost all trust in her and finally they divorced. It was now five years since she had last seen him, five years during which she had done her best to shut him out of her mind.

At first it had been hard because she truly had loved Joshua, but gradually the hurt and the love faded. She'd been a fool to get married so young, a fool to follow her heart instead of her head. But now she was older and wiser, and even if her heart had skipped a few beats at the sight of Joshua it didn't mean that she felt anything for him. And he clearly had no time for her. He couldn't wait to get back to England.

'Are you expecting me to run the vineyard single-handed while you reap a share of the profits?' she asked him coolly, wishing her mother and Steve hadn't put her in this position. They should have known there was no point. If she and Joshua hadn't patched up their differences after all these years it was hardly likely they would do so now. Forcing them together was the worst thing they could have done.

'I wouldn't do that,' he replied coolly. 'As far as I'm concerned you can have the lot.'

'Good,' she snapped. 'I'd have been saved a whole heap of trouble if they'd left you money the same as they did Mark. I don't know what they thought they were doing.'

'Of course you know.' He gave a brief, cynical smile. 'But don't worry, you won't have to do a thing. I'll simply transfer my half of the estate to you.'

'It's not what they wanted,' she demurred, mentally shaking her head. During the funeral, and the days leading up to it, she'd been in such a daze that she had hardly taken in the fact that Joshua had been her sole support. He had taken care of most of the arrangements, always there when she needed him, whether it was as a shoulder to cry on or to sort out what had seemed at the time to be insurmountable problems. Now the numbness was wearing off and she was beginning to realise just how much she owed him.

'Maybe,' he agreed, 'but it's hardly a tolerable situation for either of us. Added to the fact that I know nothing about making wine. You're far better equipped to take over.'

'I don't think you should give up your half.' Leanne had no idea what had made her say that and she wished she could take the words back. What had possessed her? She didn't want Joshua here. The very thought was abhorrent.

'Maybe I *should* stay,' he said with a reflective frown. 'It's what our respective parents wanted after all. I've long thought I should diversify. Mark can look after things in London while I find out all I can about the wine trade.'

He looked with renewed interest at the long rows of vines in front of them, the green of the foliage standing out in stark contrast to the reddish-brown earth. 'I owe it to my father. He was very taken with your country; he couldn't stop singing its praises. He invited me over many times.'

Leanne felt her heart dip. 'And we both know that I was the reason you never came. So why change your mind now? It's not necessary for you to take an active part.'

'I think it's what was meant.'

'Of course,' she agreed, 'but they were a pair of romantics. They could never accept that we'd split up for good.'

'Have there been any other men in your life?'

It was a question she hadn't expected and didn't want to answer. Her traumatic experience with Joshua had put her off men. She didn't want to get seriously involved with anyone.

He turned and studied her, those deep blue eyes that she remembered so well searching every corner of her face. 'You're a very attractive lady. If anything you're even more beautiful than you were when I met you. I can't see you ever being short of admirers.'

'I'm not,' she returned crisply.

'But you're not telling me whether there's anyone special?'

'No.'

'Then I take it there's no one. Good. At least I know where I stand.'

Leanne frowned. 'What do you mean?' He didn't stand anywhere; he was no longer a part of her life. He'd let her down when he took his brother's word against hers, and she'd hoped never to see him again.

'Guys don't like it when ex-husbands appear on the scene.'

'Even when they're no threat?' she jeered.

'Even then. They can get jealous; things can turn ugly.'

'The way they did when Mark told lies about me?' She flashed him a look of pure hatred. 'When's he going home?' Mark had turned up for the funeral the day before Joshua and behaved as though nothing had happened. He had the hide of a rhinoceros, she'd decided, and it had only been out of a sense of loyalty to Pauline and Steve and the sadness of the occasion that she hadn't given him a piece of her mind.

'Tomorrow, I believe,' he answered with a narrowed glance in her direction. 'There's no reason for him to remain—unless you'd like him to, of course?'

It was a loaded question and Leanne didn't even deign to answer. She turned away and began walking towards the house. It bothered her that Joshua was going to stay; it would be an untenable situation.

Up until now she hadn't really decided what she was going to do; whether she was going to hang on to the winery or sell. She certainly hadn't expected Joshua to be left half of it, and for him to now declare that he intended learning the ropes and helping her run it didn't please her at all.

It was her own fault, she supposed, for saying that their parents wouldn't have wanted him to give up his half. She ought to have kept her mouth shut. Hopefully, though, he wouldn't like it. He would miss London too much and head back in a very short space of time.

She came to a sudden halt as Mark blocked her path. 'Did Josh tell you I'm leaving tomorrow?' Mark was shorter than his brother, but his hair was the same polished black, and his eyes were a similar blue.

Leanne nodded.

'He hasn't said whether he's coming too?'

'No, so you'd best ask him yourself,' she snapped.

His brows rose. 'It looks as though my dear brother has upset you again. I saw you talking; I'd hoped you would kiss and make up.'

'Really?' asked Leanne crossly.

'It's been a long time. I hadn't realised you still bore a grudge. You look adorable.' He laid his hand on her arm. 'Can you forgive?'

'Not ever,' she slammed, snatching away. 'How could I possibly forgive you for telling Joshua that I'd slept with you? And how can I forgive him for believing you?'

'That's a pity.' Mark didn't seem at all put out by

her sharp words, trailing his fingers in a deliberately sensual gesture across her cheek. 'My brother still holds a candle for you, do you know that?'

'Very funny,' she retorted. 'Is that why he divorced me? Why he's kept away all these years?'

'He was angry.'

'And I don't suppose you ever told him the truth?'

'And he has his pride,' he added, evading her question.

Which meant that Mark had said nothing. She hadn't really expected him to. It wasn't on his agenda to put himself in a bad light.

From the moment they met Mark had zoned in on her, appearing unconcerned that she was Joshua's girlfriend. At first she had been very polite towards him, not wishing to cause any friction, but as time went by and he showed no sign of losing interest, not even when they married, she had deliberately turned the cold shoulder. But even this had not worked; in fact, it had seemed to make him even more determined.

She could have told Joshua—he would have had a word with him—but surely she was woman enough to handle Mark? And yet she had never known anyone more persistent.

He was actually quite a nice guy on the surface. Everyone liked him; he was good-looking and fun and she knew that no one would believe her if she told them that he kept making passes at her. They would think that she was encouraging him.

'How's Sandra?' she asked him now, more out of politeness than because she was interested. Her parents had gone over for the wedding but she had declined. She hadn't been able to face meeting either of the two Powers brothers again. There was so much anger and hostility in her that she knew it would have all come pouring out and spoiled the joyous occasion.

'She's well. The baby's due any day now.'

'Then let's hope you make it home in time. It's a shame your father will never see his first grandchild.'

He nodded and seemed about to say something else when Joshua joined them. 'What's this, a cosy little get-together?' he asked, his eyes glittering from her to his brother.

He must have seen Mark touch her, thought Leanne; perhaps he even thought that she'd invited it? Sickened to the depths of her stomach, she turned away. 'I apologise if speaking to your brother is a sin,' she spat coldly. 'Excuse me, I have things to do.'

As she walked towards the house Courtney ran out and flung herself at Leanne. 'I couldn't find you.'

Leanne hugged her three-year-old sister. 'I wasn't far away. I was talking to Joshua.'

It had been such a shock when Pauline announced that she was pregnant. At the age of forty-two Leanne had thought her mother would have no more children. And now Courtney was clinging to her hand and dragging her inside the house. 'Come and play with me, Leanne. Come and play.'

Leanne didn't see Joshua again until dinnertime. She had already bathed Courtney and put her to bed, reading quietly to her, not stopping until the grip on her hand relaxed, telling her that the child was asleep.

Joshua was sitting on the veranda where purple bougainvillaea rambled prettily along its rails. The heat of the day had relented and it was pleasantly warm. It was the time that Leanne loved best and she spent hours out here with a book or her thoughts—or at least she had done until the tragic accident. It was hard to sit quietly now. Her whole life had been turned upside-down. The death of her father had been bad enough, but now that her mother and stepfather were gone too she found it hard to accept that her life would ever get back to normal. And she didn't even have a man to share her thoughts with.

Not, she told herself strictly, that she intended feeling sorry for herself. Life had to go on. She'd got over things in the past; she would get over this. Except that if Joshua made his home here it would be doubly difficult. Would he stay at the house with her? Or would he find a place of his own? She prayed it would be the latter.

'You were a long time settling Courtney.' He looked up as she stood in the doorway and she found his searching blue eyes extremely unnerving. He'd always had the power to melt her bones with a mere glance, to make her give way to her emotions and press her body close to his, inviting him to make love. But this was different.

It sent an electric impulse through her, yes, but it was hatred that set her emotions on fire now. She prayed from the bottom of her heart that he would change his mind and fly home with his brother. After showering she had pulled on a black flowered gypsy skirt and top and with her hands pushed into the deep pockets she kept her fingers well and truly crossed.

'I was about to come and see if I could help,' he said.

Leanne smiled wryly. 'She's afraid to be on her own. Her world's fallen apart. She thinks that if she lets me out of her sight she'll lose me too.'

Joshua nodded. 'All the more reason why I should spend time here. It's too much for you to cope with alone.'

He didn't mean that, she felt sure; it was their baby sister he was thinking of. He idolised Courtney as much as she adored him. Each year since she'd been born Pauline and Steve had taken their tiny offspring to England and Courtney had vivid memories of Josh. She would be in her element if he was to stay here now.

'I was thinking of selling the winery.'

Joshua looked at her sharply. 'Where did that idea come from?'

CHAPTER TWO

'I DON'T know,' Leanne answered honestly. She hadn't even thought about selling; it was far too early to make such a decision. She hadn't the interest her parents had had in the winery, and she did have a job, but with Courtney to look after she knew that she would have to give it up. And if she sold the winery, where would her income come from? Her share wouldn't last forever. There was money in trust for Courtney but the child couldn't touch that until she was twenty-one, so it would be up to her to bring up her young sister.

She needed the security of the winery. And maybe if Joshua took over the running of it, it would leave her with free time to look after Courtney. So long as he didn't live here in this house. Compared to his London home it wasn't very grand, although it did have five bedrooms. Only the main room had its own shower room, though, and there was one family bathroom. Steve had kept promising to put *en suites* into all of the bedrooms but never got round to it. In fact the whole place needed modernising.

It was a low, wide building, with a veranda running around all sides. There were orange and peach trees in the garden and her mother had grown parsnips and tomatoes and eggplants, as well as a whole host of other vegetables and herbs. There was also a pool, though at this moment it was very much in need of a clean-up.

Trying to look at it all from a stranger's eyes, Leanne realised it wasn't very impressive, though to her it meant everything. It was home, it was where she had been born and spent her whole life—except for that disastrous couple of years in England!

In contrast the winery buildings were modern and up-to-date and Hugh Lindsay Wines were fast becoming a household name. She was proud of what her father had started, and it would, she knew, be wrong of her to sell.

'I think we should give it a go,' said Joshua firmly. 'I want you to teach me everything you know, right from the growing of the grapes, to the harvesting, the fermenting, the bottling; everything.'

Leanne grimaced. 'I think Ivan Eldridge—he was my father's right-hand man—is far better equipped to do that than me. I only play at it. I have my own job.'

'Which is?' he asked with a frown.

'I'm a computer programmer.'

'Since when?'

'Since I came back here.'

'But before that you helped your parents?'

'Well, yes, but when my mother remarried Steve was so keen, and so able, that I felt surplus to requirements. Not that either of them would ever have said that, but actually it was good to get out and meet other people.'

'You were hankering for male company, is that it?' he enquired with narrowed eyes.

Leanne knew what he was thinking and quick anger

flooded her veins. 'Actually, yes,' she lied. 'And I've met plenty in the course of my job.'

'How many have you bedded?' The question was shot with the precision of a blow dart in the hands of an expert.

'Too many to count,' she declared fiercely. It was what he expected; why should she tell him that no one had ever filled her with such deep and precious feelings as she had experienced with him? Not that her feelings were deep and precious any longer. Deep, yes; precious, no. Deeply angry, deeply disappointed, deeply hurt.

In fact her whole body was filled with an all-consuming hatred. Over the years her feelings had faded; she had thought herself over him. But when he turned up for the funeral the whole gamut of emotions had erupted back into life.

He studied her face long and hard, no expression at all in his midnight-dark eyes, and then he turned away.

'Dinner's ready,' she said quietly.

A neighbour, a close friend of her mother, was helping until Leanne had sorted herself out, and it was Molly who had cooked the meal now. But sitting at the table with Joshua and Mark was an ordeal Leanne could have done without. After Joshua's earlier remark she was almost frightened to look at Mark.

'I've decided,' said Joshua to his brother, 'to stay on for a while.'

'I guessed you would,' said Mark, 'now that you have a vested interest. I wish you luck.' He hadn't been at all put out that he hadn't been left a share. It wasn't his cup of tea, he had said. He much preferred living in London. Besides which, he'd be in charge of things there now.

Mark had visibly grown in stature when he said that. Perhaps it would be the making of him, thought Leanne. That and the fact that he had a wife and a child on the way. It must be hard being the second son. It was probably what had made him behave as he had. And why was she defending him when he had ruined her marriage?

The crunch had come when he'd called at the apartment one day and tried to kiss her. 'Why is it my brother always gets the best girls?' he'd asked bitterly.

'It could be because he's gentle and kind,' she'd retorted. 'Let me go, Mark.'

'Joshua, gentle? I don't think so,' he derided. 'You clearly don't know him very well yet. And when you do I guarantee your marriage won't last. He's had girlfriends galore; I bet he hasn't told you that. You're the first idiot who's agreed to marry him.'

'He loves me,' she defended. 'And I love him.'

'Love?' he returned scornfully. 'Neither of you knows the meaning of the word. I'll show you what love's all about,' and he clamped his lips down so hard on hers that it hurt. And no matter how much she fought Leanne couldn't free herself. She was fighting for breath by the time he released her, and she was a bundle of fury as she rained her fists on his chest.

'How dare you?' she shrieked. 'How dare you? I've put up with you molesting me long enough. I'm going to tell Joshua; he'll put a stop to it.'

He laughed into her face. 'You won't do that; you

know you won't. You'd have done it long before now
if you felt that strongly. You're simply scared because
I arouse you far more deeply than my brother ever
has. Come on, let's go to bed. He'll never find out.
Let me teach you what it's like to be made love to
by a real man.'

Taking her arm, he began to drag her out of the
room, but Leanne swung around and with her free
hand slapped him as hard as she could across the face.
'Let me go, you brute.'

His eyes had narrowed, blue eyes so very much
like his brother's, but they never darkened with desire
or softened with love. 'You'll regret that, I assure
you,' he'd warned.

'And you'll regret ever touching me,' she'd lashed
out.

She dashed the thoughts away now and tried to
concentrate on what Joshua was saying.

'I'm looking forward to the challenge,' he told
Mark. 'Leanne's going to teach me all she knows, and
the rest I'll gain by hands-on experience.'

No, I'm not, Leanne silently protested, but she
didn't want to cause any unpleasantness before Mark
left. She gave Joshua a weak smile instead. 'I'm
warning you, my knowledge is very limited.'

'I don't believe that,' he said. 'How long's the
vineyard been going now? Twenty years?'

'Don't forget I was a child for most of those,' she
declared.

'You're being modest. I bet you could run things
single-handed.'

'I don't have the interest my parents had,' she
pointed out.

'Which will change now that you're a co-owner.'

She lifted her brows as she looked at him. 'I wouldn't be too sure.'

'Because you resent me owning an equal share?'

'I resent you being here, full stop,' she tossed back swiftly. 'It's futile. It won't bring us back together, it will simply make life unbearable for both of us. I can't see it working.'

'Not if you continue to hold that attitude.' His eyes stabbed fiercely into hers, sending tiny shock waves through her body. In that instant Leanne realised that not all her feelings were dead.

It was a terrible discovery. How could she even feel a flicker of sensation after what he had done to her? It was ridiculous. 'How do you expect me to behave?' she asked heatedly, her green eyes full of fire.

'I think our parents would want you to respect their wishes. All we have to do is work together. I don't want to share your bed again, if that's what's worrying you.'

Ouch! He couldn't have made it any clearer that he no longer desired her. And although it was exactly what she needed to hear it was still like a slap across the face. No girl liked to be told that she was no longer attractive. 'The thought never crossed my mind. You mean nothing to me,' she snapped.

He'd meant nothing since the day of their showdown. The whole sorry scene came flashing back.

'What have you and Mark been up to?' asked Joshua on arriving home.

It was the same day that Mark had made his threat

and Leanne shivered now, wondering what he'd said to his brother.

'What do you mean, what we've been up to? Mark's done nothing but try and get me to bed ever since I met him. He's a creep of the worst kind. I didn't want to say anything because he's your brother, but—'

'I bet you didn't want to say anything,' he sneered, 'because you were the one chasing Mark. How could I have been taken in by you? Get out of my house!'

Leanne staggered backwards as though he had struck her. Mark had cleverly turned the tables. 'What's he said to you?' she asked, her voice trembling with fear. She loved this man with every fibre of her being and had no intention of letting his devious brother split them up.

'Enough to let me know what kind of a girl I'm married to,' he lashed.

'He's lying,' she retorted hotly. 'He's lying to save his own face because I threatened to tell you what he was up to.'

'And I'm expected to believe that?' Hard eyes searched hers. 'I should have seen this coming. I've observed the two of you together and I was pleased that you were getting on so well. Pleased, dammit!' He smashed his hand down on the edge of the table. 'What a blind fool I've been. What did you think, that you'd have the best of both worlds?'

Leanne shivered. He was cutting her to ribbons. 'Joshua, listen to me,' she pleaded. 'It's not like that. Mark—'

'I'm supposed to believe you, whom I've known

for little more than twelve months, against my own brother?' he stormed. 'Don't fool yourself, Leanne.'

'But I didn't do anything,' she protested. 'I've tried to fight Mark off. I've never led him on; I wouldn't do that. I love you. I love you so much, Joshua; you must believe me.'

He closed his eyes, shutting her out as effectively as if he had left the room and Leanne didn't know what to do to make him believe her. She could understand him wanting to believe his brother, but she was his wife, for heaven's sake. Were his feelings so fickle that he didn't trust her? 'I want to see Mark,' she said loudly. 'We need to talk about this, the three of us.'

'You think that will make any difference?' he asked cuttingly.

'I'm your wife.' Her eyes flashed a brilliant, angry green. 'A man should trust his wife. I trust you. I wouldn't believe anyone if they told me you'd committed adultery, certainly not if you told me otherwise. And I'm telling you, Joshua, I have never been to bed with Mark; I've never encouraged him; I've spent all my time fighting him off.'

'It's strange he should say the same about you, don't you think?' he jeered. 'I reckon I've been blind and stupid all these months.'

'Joshua, please,' she pleaded, laying her hand on his arm, but he thrust her savagely away. 'I'll fetch Mark myself,' she yelled. 'I refuse to let him ruin our marriage.'

Joshua spread his hands expressively. 'Feel free.'

And so Leanne telephoned Mark and asked him to come over.

'The bomb's gone off, has it?' he asked quietly, and she could hear the smile in his voice. In that instant she realised that his coming would do no good. Mark had sown the seeds of evil and they would continue to flourish in Joshua's mind no matter what she said.

Her prophecy proved correct. Mark swore that she had done all the running and Joshua believed him. The next day, after further heated words with her husband, Leanne left the apartment and she hadn't seen Joshua again until he came over for the funeral.

She glared at him now across the table.

'Maybe we can come to some agreement regarding running the vineyard?' he suggested.

'And I think maybe I should leave you two to sort out your problems,' said Mark, getting up. 'I have my packing to finish.'

'There's no need,' she said at once. 'Josh and I can have this conversation any time. It was rude of us to talk business when—'

Mark's lips quirked. 'Actually I'd like to go before the boxing gloves come out.'

'It won't get that far,' said Joshua coolly. 'Leanne is beginning to realise that she has no choice.'

Her head jerked up and her eyes flashed but before she could speak Mark said calmly, 'I'll go.'

And as soon as he had left the room she let fly. 'How dare you say I have no choice? Who the hell do you think you are? This was my family business long before you and your father came on the scene.' And, dammit, why did he look so relaxed? He was even smiling, he was so sure of himself. She wanted to wipe it off his face; she wanted to strike him; she wanted to beat her fists against his chest. God, she detested this man.

'And now it is half mine,' he answered calmly. 'You may as well accept the fact.'

She couldn't, not ever. 'You could do the decent thing and get out of my life.'

The self-satisfied smile lifted one corner of his mouth. 'In a perfect world that's what I'd do, isn't it? But I'm afraid we don't live in a perfect world. You're stuck with the situation, like it or not.'

Leanne picked up her wine glass and took a long swallow of the pale amber Riesling. 'I despise you, Joshua Powers.'

'I can't say I'm too impressed with a wife who's slept with her husband's brother either, but it's up to us to make the most of a bad situation. Your mother made my father very happy. He loved it here, he loved Australia, he loved what he was doing; he never stopped telling me. We both owe it to our respective parents to uphold the name of Hugh Lindsay Wines. We owe it to Courtney too.'

Grudgingly she had to admit that he was right, but it would be hard. She took another mouthful of wine, one of their own, naturally, savouring the fruity flavour, and she knew in that moment that she couldn't let her mother down. One way or another she had to work with Joshua to keep the winery running.

Joshua hated the idea of them working together as much as Leanne did. Their parents had put them in an intolerable situation, but only because they'd had their best interests at heart.

His father had been desolate when their marriage fell apart, as had Leanne's mother, and every time they came home to England they'd put pressure on him to make up. They hadn't realised how impossible it was. He couldn't forgive infidelity, not ever. His marriage vows had been for life, and at the time he'd been sure Leanne felt the same. So why, then, had she turned to his brother?

Not that it was the first time his brother had made advances to whichever girl he happened to be dating. It had become a pastime with him, as if trying to prove that he was the better man. And if the girl in question was foolish enough to go off with his brother then it proved to Joshua that she wasn't the one for him.

But he had thought Leanne was different. She had been young, admittedly, when they married, and probably open to flattery. But she had professed to love him deeply and swore there would never be any other man. So why had she carried on an affair with Mark?

Because he, Joshua, couldn't satisfy her? Was that it? He had tossed the thought back and forth in his mind until it had become contorted and evil. It wasn't a good feeling knowing that his own wife preferred another man. It had done nothing for his morale and he had sunk into the lowest abyss of his life. In fact he'd been heartbroken, not that he would ever have admitted it to anyone, but in the dark of the night there had been moments when tears slid down his cheeks.

It had taken him months to crawl out. He'd put on a brave face and carried on as though nothing was wrong, and he'd vowed to himself that he would never let the same thing happen again. He'd also sworn that if he ever did come face to face with Leanne he would cut her dead. What he hadn't expected was to be thrust into this situation.

When Leanne had phoned to tell him about the bush fire that had taken his father's and her mother's life he had been too stunned to say much, his only thought that he had to get over there fast. He had found her in such a state that not only had he needed to console her, but he'd had to deal with everything else as well. It had been a difficult time for everyone.

But now, with the funeral over and life needing to get back to normal, or as near to normal as it could be under the circumstances, he had made the decision to stay and help run the business. Neither of them were happy about it but he felt a very strong need to honour their parents' wishes.

He was looking forward to learning the business, and hopefully improving it. It was what he did best. He had the eye to see things that others didn't. He loved a challenge.

His image was of a laid-back sort of guy, and he liked to cultivate that, but inside he had a core of steel. And if he wanted to help turn what was, according to Leanne, an already profitable company into an even better one, then it was his duty to stay and take over his share.

This was Courtney's inheritance; he was doing it as much for her as for himself. He was extremely fond of his tiny sister, and if his marriage had worked out he and Leanne might have had a child of their own around the same age. It hurt when this thought passed through his mind, as it had so many times in the past, and he couldn't help laying the blame on Leanne.

'So—are you agreeable that we give it a go?' he asked tersely.

Leanne nodded and, her wine gone, she put the glass down. 'Where do you plan on living?'

'Why, here of course.' What did she think, that he'd move out? Not likely; he needed to be on hand. 'And you, will you give up your job?'

'I have little choice if I want to keep my eye on what you're doing.' Her beautiful, wide-spaced eyes were steady on his, as if she was expecting him to come back with some sharp rejoinder. He didn't give her the pleasure.

'An excellent decision,' he said instead. 'I think one of us should take the master bedroom—then we won't both be vying for bathroom space.' There had been an occasion when he'd gone to use the bathroom, only to find it occupied by Leanne. He'd blithely walked in just as she was stepping out of the shower. She'd shrieked as though he were a stranger and snatched up a towel.

'You're hiding nothing I haven't seen before,' he'd tossed lightly, amused by her response. She was as exquisite as the day he'd married her—long, shapely legs, a tiny waist and high, pert breasts that simply begged to be touched. Her movements were fluid and graceful, despite her haste, and he hadn't been able to stop a swift hormonal surge. He'd quickly assured himself that it was a natural reaction when confronted by an exceptionally pretty nude woman; nothing at all to do with the fact that he had once been in love with her.

'You can have it,' she said swiftly. 'Courtney's used to the other bathroom; I don't want to disturb her routine.'

'Of course not.' He kept his smile well hidden. 'I'll move my things tomorrow. And after that you can show me around the estate.'

Although initially he hadn't intended staying in Australia, although he knew that he would never forgive Leanne, he was in fact looking forward to helping her run the business. It could be a mistake living in the same house, it could be hell as there was no love lost between them, but he was willing to take that chance.

'Lord knows what the reason is,' bemoaned Mark over breakfast the following morning, 'but it means I'm stuck here for another day. How can they cancel flights like that? I have a wife who needs me. What if she goes into early labour? What if—'

'All the what-ifs in the world will make no difference,' Joshua told him calmly. 'Stop panicking.'

'It's easy for you to say that; you've never been an expectant father.'

'Nor am I likely to be,' came the swift answer.

So Joshua had no intention of getting married again. Leanne was surprised. He was the sort of man who could have any girl he wanted. Her mother had told her that he was seeing someone. What had happened to her? Not that she was interested; not in the slightest. It was just odd that he had chosen to remain single again for so long.

Mark accompanied them on their tour of the vineyards, though Leanne could see that he had no real interest. It was simply better than doing nothing. Joshua on the other hand asked innumerable questions, taking notes, showing a voracious appetite for everything. Even when it was time for lunch he showed no sign of wanting to take a break.

'My brother's such a workaholic,' said Mark in a bored voice. 'How about you and me going back to the house? Will Molly have lunch ready?'

Leanne nodded. 'Joshua?'

'What?' He was preoccupied.

'Are you ready to eat?'

'Not yet.'

'Then we'll go on ahead,' said Mark. 'I'm starving.'

Leanne wasn't sure which brother she wanted to be with. Neither, if the truth were known. She hated them both with equal intensity.

'Joshua really is taking this wine-making thing seriously, isn't he?' Courtney, who had been looked after by Molly all morning, was now having her midday nap, and they were sitting on the shady veranda enjoying the salad and sandwiches Molly had prepared. In the distance the vines were green and lush, the grapes almost ready for harvesting. And closer to the house deep red roses still bloomed, spilling their heady scent into the air.

Leanne nodded.

'I never thought anything would get him away from London and his work there. It's his whole life. To tell you the truth I'm glad of the opportunity to look after things myself. Much as I love my brother, I resent the way he rarely lets me make decisions.'

'If he thinks he's going to take over here he's very

much mistaken,' said Leanne quickly. 'Ivan Eldridge is in charge. He won't take kindly to a stranger telling him what to do, especially someone who doesn't know the industry inside out, even though he is the new boss. Or one of them,' she added quickly.

Mark gave a wry smile. 'You don't know Josh very well, then. He'll know everything in no time at all. He has the sharpest brain of anyone I know. Surely you learned that much when you were married?'

Leanne shrugged. 'He never brought his work home.'

'You were still at the honeymoon stage, eh? And I ruined it. If it's any consolation I've regretted it ever since. More especially since I got married. It was a dreadful thing to do. Can you ever forgive me?'

'I doubt it,' said Leanne honestly. 'On the other hand I can't forgive Josh either. Why didn't he believe me when I said you were lying?'

'Because I was convincing, too good a liar, I guess. I was a first-class swine in those days, and I know it. And, having seen you two together again, I'm even more consumed with guilt.'

Leanne frowned. 'There's no need. You probably did me a favour. Trust has a big part to play in a marriage and if he couldn't trust me then he wasn't the man for me.'

Mark shook his head, his expression sceptical. 'I'm not so sure; I've seen the way he looks at you in unguarded moments. Not that he's ever said anything, of course; Josh wouldn't. But even so—'

'Nonsense,' cut in Leanne sharply. 'In any case, I don't love him any more.'

'So why haven't you found yourself some other

nice guy? And why hasn't Josh found himself another wife? I thought he was being wary, too wary in my opinion. But now I know that there'll never be anyone else for him but you.'

'You're talking rubbish.' Leanne gave him a furious flash of her green eyes.

'I don't think so.' Mark took another bite of his chicken and avocado sandwich, and after chewing thoughtfully for a second said, 'I think I ought to put matters straight before I go. I think I should tell him the truth. It's a bit late, I know, but better late than never, isn't that what they say?'

'Don't you dare!' warned Leanne hotly. 'What's done is done; I don't want him crawling to me.' And then she laughed. The vision of Joshua eating humble pie was ludicrous. And clearly Mark thought the same because he joined in her laughter.

'Can I share the joke?'

Neither of them had seen or heard Joshua approach, and there was no amusement in his eyes when Leanne looked at him. In fact they were as hard as the sapphires they reflected. It didn't take much working out to realise that he thought she and Mark were getting too cosy again—and of course she couldn't tell him what they were laughing about.

'It's nothing you'd appreciate,' Mark said. 'But you're in the nick of time. Grab a sandwich before I eat them all.'

'I'm not hungry,' Joshua growled, and after a further condemning glare in Leanne's direction he strode into the house.

'He's jealous,' said Mark softly.

'Don't be stupid,' returned Leanne.

When she took the empty plates into the kitchen later she found Joshua sitting in the rocking chair with Courtney on his lap, telling her a very silly story about a kitten that could fly. She paused a moment in the doorway, entranced at the sight of this tall, cross man cuddling her little sister and speaking in gentle tones, changing his voice to a squeak when it was the kitten's turn to say something. Courtney giggled constantly and when the story ended she implored him to tell her another.

It was only then that he noticed Leanne. Immediately he set Courtney on her feet. 'Another time, sweetheart. I have to go back to work.' And he swept past Leanne without a word.

CHAPTER THREE

'TOMORROW we begin harvesting.'

Leanne looked sharply at Joshua over the dinner table. Mark had left early that morning and she'd spent the day with Courtney while Joshua had gone to the winery again. She hadn't felt the need to go with him. Ivan could explain all he needed to know.

It wasn't the fact that he knew before her what they were going to do that bothered her, but the fact that he'd said 'we', as though he was already a big part of the company. In essence he was, but in a learning sense he wasn't.

'And you're going to help?' she asked sharply.

His brows rose, untidy brows that she had sometimes stroked to try and restore order. They had always rigidly refused. She had teased him that they were made of wire. 'What's wrong? Missing Mark, are you?' he goaded. 'Is that why you're out of sorts?'

'I'm not—out of sorts, I mean. It's just that you're talking as though you already know as much as Ivan.'

'I'm learning.'

'Theory and practice are two different things.'

'You'd rather I fell flat on my face and returned to London. Is that it?'

'Not at all,' she assured him, though in truth it was what she wanted. It was already proving traumatic having him live in the same house. Half of her remembered the good times they'd had together, while the other half, the predominant half, could only recall that he had cold-heartedly thrown her out of his life. And that was something she could never forget or forgive.

'Do you know,' he said, leaning back in his chair and looking at her with the lopsided smile that had once set her heart racing, 'I wasn't so sure that I would enjoy living here but already I'm beginning to feel at home. I can see why my father loved it. It's a great country.'

'Don't you miss England? London in particular?'

'I thought I would, but actually no. When I first came out, when I learned that my father had died, I felt quite sure that it would hold such terrible memories for me that I wouldn't be able to wait to go home. But surprisingly that's not the case.'

After a moment's pause, when he seemed to be deep in thought, he added, 'I know we haven't spoken about it much, but I really would like to know more about the fire that killed our parents.'

Leanne clenched her fingers into fists and balled them under her chin, looking down at her lap, reliving those vivid memories that had caused her such grief. 'I thought you knew.'

'Not the details.'

Her hurt was still so raw that she found it difficult to speak and several long seconds passed before she could begin. 'We had a holiday home in Northern Queensland, in a small town on the edge of the bush. We spent most of my school holidays there. It wasn't much of a place, a shack really, but we loved it. We'd explore the river that ran near by, and we'd fish, and sometimes we'd take a tent and go camping. It was lots of fun. My mother wanted your father to see it. They planned a week's holiday.' Her voice broke but she managed to go on.

'Some nearby campers were careless with cigarettes. In no time the whole area, including the town, was on fire. Our parents were the only two who didn't escape. Our house was nearest to the fire, you see. They had no warning, no time to...'

Tears streamed down her cheeks and suddenly Joshua's chair was drawn up close to hers and she was in his arms. 'I'm sorry, I didn't mean to upset you,' he said, dabbing at her face with a handkerchief. 'It was important to me that I knew. I'd put off asking earlier because—'

'It's all right,' Leanne managed to choke out. 'It's all right.'

'No, it's not. I'm an insensitive brute. I could have asked someone else; I didn't have to ask you. I'm sorry.'

Leanne buried her head in his shoulder, feeling the warmth and strength of this man who had once been her husband, whom she'd loved more deeply than she had ever thought possible. He had been her dream man, perfect in every way. How could it have all gone so wrong?

She didn't move until her tears had dried and even then she didn't want to. She felt comforted, as he had comforted her when he first came out. He meant nothing by it, she realised that, but even so it felt good in his arms. It was hard being strong all by herself.

And then amazingly other, different feelings began to insinuate themselves. A crazy kind of excitement because he was one hell of a sexy man. It didn't matter that he had once banished her from his life, the feelings were there. Those selfsame feelings she had experienced when they first met. Dangerous feelings!

With a speed born of desperation she brushed his arms aside and jumped up. 'I have to check on Courtney.'

She was furiously angry with herself and as she bolted for her bedroom Leanne blamed Joshua for what had happened. Why had he touched her? What was he playing at? Didn't he realise that she hated his very soul? She didn't want him to comfort her, she wanted him to keep well away. She didn't even want to talk to him. Why had their parents done this? Why had they thrust them together? Hadn't they realised the problems it would cause? The torment? The heartache?

Joshua sat quietly after Leanne had gone, the horror of the situation she had just described going round and round in his mind. Many long minutes passed before he told himself that there was no point in dwelling on it. His father would want him to get on with his life, as would Leanne's mother, and the best way to do that was by making a continuing success of the vineyard.

His lips twisted bitterly as he recalled the way Leanne had rushed away and he would love to know what was going on inside her head. Courtney was an excuse, he was aware of that. It was either the distress of the situation or the fact that she couldn't bear to be touched by him. Probably the latter. The thought hurt; it hurt deeply.

He'd reflected long and hard about the break-up of

their marriage, unable to understand why or how he had misjudged her so badly. Or maybe he had seen the signs and refused to recognise them.

Joshua's lips closed grimly now and he pushed himself to his feet and left the dining room, his meal almost untouched. Unable to relax, he paced the veranda for a few minutes then strode away from the house. For over an hour he walked, finding the peace he needed between the rows of vines.

This was where his father had created a new life for himself, where he had been happier than he'd been for years, and Joshua began to feel the same sense of pleasure and satisfaction. It was cool and calming, and the vital signs of life all around him seemed to somehow insinuate themselves into his body.

When he finally got back to the house Ivan Eldridge was there. He and Leanne were sitting on the veranda enjoying a glass of wine and laughing easily together. Ivan was a big, bluff man in his early thirties, with a ruddy complexion and hair so blond that it was almost white.

Joshua hadn't realised how friendly he and Leanne were, and he stood for a moment in the shadow of a ghost gum, watching them. They were completely relaxed in each other's company and Joshua felt a pang of something very akin to jealousy. He dismissed it instantly—he wasn't jealous, he couldn't be—but the thought remained as he walked towards them, his eyes narrowed and assessing.

'Joshua,' said Ivan at once, jumping up. 'There's a day's delay with the harvesting; most of the pickers can't make it until Thursday.'

'It's good of you to let me know,' said Joshua, not

at all sure that this was the real reason he had come
to the house. 'But I'll probably be there anyway. I'm
thirsty for knowledge. I'll spend time in the office.
It's about time I looked at the books. And you ought
to come too, Leanne,' he added as an afterthought, as
though suddenly remembering that she was his partner.

'There's no need to bore yourself silly with stuff
like that,' said Ivan at once.

'I won't find it boring,' Joshua assured him.
'There's always room for improvement; people don't
realise that. What computer programme do you run?'

Ivan shrugged. 'None at all. We use the computer
mainly for letters and invoices. Mainly we stick to the
old paperwork methods introduced by Leanne's father. It worked well for him; it's working for us now.
It's an easy, simple method and I can do most of it
myself. Pauline used to help but I'm perfectly capable. We have a girl in at the end of each month to do
some of the accounts.'

'I see,' said Joshua. 'I'll still take a look, though.'
He tried to make it sound as though it wasn't much
of a big deal, but from his vast experience of studying
other people's working methods he felt sure that he
could come up with something to make things run
more smoothly and easily. Not that he wanted to tread
on Ivan's shoes at this early stage. 'And with Leanne
being a computer programmer these days,' he added,
'we might be able to make things a lot easier all
round. I'm surprised you've never thought of it yourself, Leanne.'

He looked where she sat on one of the old canvas
chairs, cold resentment in her eyes. 'When Mum and

Steve were running the business I never interfered,'
she told him coolly.

'It's not interfering, it's good management. And as
the vineyard now belongs to you and me I see it as
the perfect excuse to modernise.'

'I think,' she said tartly, casting a look at Ivan's
agonised face, 'that you're trying to run before you
can walk. You need to learn the business properly
before you mess around with the records.'

He shrugged easily. 'Maybe you're right.' But it
didn't mean he wouldn't take a look as soon as he
got the opportunity.

Once harvesting began Leanne didn't see much of
Joshua. He was there with his bucket, picking with
the rest of them, which surprised her. It oughtn't to
have done because she knew that Joshua liked to learn
first-hand every part of a process before making any
changes. It was the only way, he had once told her.

She didn't go back to her job, phoning and explaining her situation, relieved when they understood. She
spent her time running the house and looking after
her little sister. Courtney had no hang-ups where
Joshua was concerned and she couldn't wait for him
to come home each evening so that she could climb
onto his lap and be told a story. He was very good
with her and Leanne enjoyed watching them together.
How easy it was for children to accept people. Joshua
was Mr Nice Guy personified as far as Courtney was
concerned.

Most evenings, when Courtney was in bed and the
sun had gone down after another crucifyingly hot day,
Leanne and Joshua sat out on the veranda. They

talked about all sorts of things. What he'd learned, the differences between this life and the one he'd left, world affairs, anything and everything except themselves.

And so she was surprised when one evening he suddenly asked, 'Do you remember the day we met?'

Leanne shot him a startled glance, wondering where that had come from. How could she not remember? It had been the most sensually exciting day of her life. She could picture it now. She had gone to an eighteenth birthday party at the local golf club with one of her cousins and halfway through the evening had spotted Joshua standing at the bar.

He was older than the other partygoers and she couldn't help wondering whether he was an invited guest or a gatecrasher. Without a doubt he was the sexiest and best-looking man in the room—and he was watching her.

His hair was raven-black, shining in the light from the bar, reaching just below his ears. It needed cutting, she remembered thinking. His eyes were half closed as they studied her, making it impossible to see what colour they were. And his mouth, his lower lip sensually full, was smiling in a manner which suggested he was wondering what it would be like to make love to her.

Leanne wasn't the type of girl to jump into bed with a stranger, and yet she knew that if this guy asked she wouldn't hesitate. 'Who's that?' she enquired of her cousin.

'Oh, that's Josh. A close friend of the owners of this establishment. Everyone knows him; he's a good guy. Still looking for Miss Right, I believe. Not that he'll find her in here; we're all too young for him.'

'How old is he, then?'

Her cousin shrugged and pursed her lips. 'Who knows? Getting on for thirty, I imagine. He's ancient. Come on, drag your eyes away and dance. He's not your type.'

But every time she glanced at him he was watching her, still with that enigmatic smile. He looked so relaxed leaning back against the bar, arms lightly folded, head tilted to one side. Her whole body was fizzing inside, her mouth suddenly dry—she needed a drink, but not alcohol. Water. From the ladies' room.

As she turned the corner she found her way barred. Mr Come-to-Bed-Eyes himself.

'I've been trying to catch your eye all evening.' His voice was a low, sexy growl, intensifying the excitement that sizzled inside her.

'You have?' She pretended to be surprised, not wanting to let him know that she'd been aware of him watching her, and that he was the reason she'd scuttled away. 'Why's that?'

His lips twisted into a wry smile. 'You look lost; you don't seem to know many people here.'

His eyes were blue, a rich sapphire-blue, deep-set and sexy and mysterious. Gorgeous eyes. She could imagine looking into them as he made love to her. Gosh! Where had that thought come from? She shook her head to free it of this wild imagination. 'I don't. I came with my cousin; they're friends of hers.'

'Is that an Australian accent?' He looked at her with even closer interest.

Leanne nodded. 'I'm from South Australia, north of Adelaide.'

'The wine country?'

She was surprised that he knew. Most people she'd met in England had no idea what the region was famous for. 'That's right.'

'And what are you doing over here?'

'Visiting relatives.'

'Are you staying long?'

'A couple of months, maybe longer; I'm not sure. It's up to my mother.'

'Mmm.' His lower lip pursed and his brows drew into a quizzical frown.

Leanne's stomach muscles tightened. Such a sexy mouth. What would it be like to be kissed by him?

'Why don't we leave this party and go for a drink somewhere quiet, somewhere we can talk and get to know one another?'

Alarm bells rang. This man was far older and more experienced than she; he was also a total stranger. And yet her cousin had told her that he was well known here, a good man. Dared she risk it? She wanted to, lord knew how much. And yet she erred on the side of caution. 'I don't think so.'

'Why? I promise you no harm.'

'I don't know you; I'm sorry,' and she brushed past him and carried on to the cloakroom.

She gulped down water as though she were dying of thirst. Why had she said no when he was the most beautiful man she had ever seen? Was she the world's biggest fool? Not at all; she was simply being sensible. But she didn't want to be sensible, she wanted to take what life had to offer. She wanted to push the sadness of her father's death out of her mind. She'd never been singled out before by someone so sophisticated; it was flattering.

But she'd already told him that she wasn't interested, and he wouldn't waste his time hanging around, so why was she worrying about whether she'd done the right thing? She dragged a comb through her thick blonde hair, reapplied her lipstick, and went out again to face the world.

'You took your time.'

It was him! Waiting for her! Leaning lazily back against the wall.

'Perhaps I ought to warn you, I never take no for an answer.'

The deep, growling voice reached out and touched every nerve-end. Leanne shivered.

'But I can understand your concern, so why don't we simply find ourselves a seat somewhere and introduce ourselves?'

They had talked and talked and by the end of the evening she had agreed to go out with him. Before long they'd been lovers, and finally man and wife. And now they were single again and arch enemies.

'Of course I remember.'

'Why did you do it?'

'What? Go out with you?'

'Go to bed with my brother. Ruin everything that we had?'

Leanne jumped to her feet. 'Not that again. I don't want to talk about it; there's no point. Too much water's gone under the bridge.'

'I need to understand why you did it,' he told her

crisply. 'Fate has given me the opportunity. I think it's time to talk.'

He wouldn't listen to her before, why now? Because they'd been thrown together? Because he had no choice? Because he knew that they'd have to get along if they wanted to make a success of the winery?

'Not fate,' she spat. 'Our parents. Though actually,' she admitted, 'I don't suppose either of them thought they would die so young, so why they left the winery between us, I have no idea. I'd rather sell and share the profits. And why you want to remain and help run it is an even deeper mystery. You're not welcome, you should know that.'

'I do know it,' he retorted, his voice growing harsher by the second. He pushed himself up and although it had grown dark the light from the house spilled out onto the veranda and she could see his eyes clearly. They were hot with anger.

'But I owe it to my father and Pauline,' he went on. 'They worked hard getting the vineyard back on its feet following its months of decline. And it's beginning to go that way again. Sales aren't as good as they should be.'

'You've found this out already?' she asked sharply.

'Yes. I've looked at the books. An archaic system, I have to admit, but it's become very clear to me that marketing strategies are not what they should be. It's a case of sink or swim. A simple choice. What's it to be?'

Leanne was astonished; she'd had no idea. 'Are you sure? Ivan's a very good manager; he keeps a tight ship; he wouldn't allow this to happen.'

'Maybe he is good in certain areas, I won't dispute that. But if we're to keep the vineyard going things have to change. There's nothing wrong with the production side; it's marketing that's the problem—even the records aren't good. What I could do with is a whole new computer programme—and you're the girl to do it for me.'

'For *you*?' echoed Leanne indignantly. 'You're talking as though this whole outfit is yours alone. I think I should have some say before you make drastic changes.'

'Come and take a look for yourself, then. But believe me, I do know what I'm talking about. Will you work out a programme? Will you come with me and let me show you what needs to be done?'

Leanne drew in a deep, unhappy breath. 'I don't want to tread on Ivan's toes.'

'He means something to you, does he?' asked Joshua sharply. 'I thought you looked very cosy the other night.' His top lip curled derisively.

'We're friends, yes,' she admitted. 'Is there any crime in that?'

'He's not your type.'

'Really? And, as you're not either, what type of man do you think I should be looking for?'

Her sarcasm was lost on him. He grabbed her arms and before she could stop him his mouth claimed hers.

CHAPTER FOUR

THIS was a bad move, thought Joshua, but even so he could do nothing to stop himself. He needed to kiss Leanne, he needed to see whether any of the old spark was alive inside her.

Of one thing he was very sure. Nothing inside him had died. For years he had thought that way, he had been convinced of it, but the instant he'd seen her again he knew that there would never be anyone else for him. He'd tried, heaven alone knew he'd tried, but no one had come close to this girl he had loved and married. He even wanted to forgive her for carrying on with his brother. Though whether he could was another matter.

The feel of her mouth beneath his was setting off a chain reaction. His male hormones had suddenly become alive, his whole body on fire. And the beauty of it was that she wasn't resisting him. She wasn't exactly kissing him either, but she wasn't fighting. And this had to be a good sign.

He slid his hands behind her back, carefully, testing her reaction every inch of the way. And still she didn't move. A groan escaped from the back of his throat; he couldn't help himself. All she wore was a thin, silky top and beneath it he could feel the heat of her skin, the exquisite shape of her slender body.

He knew every inch, he had traced eager fingers over it so many times, he had kissed it so many times, he had made her uniquely his own, and now he wanted to do so again.

But although she wasn't moving, she wasn't responding either. It was as though she'd frozen into a tight, tiny ball inside herself. She was effectively shutting him out, telling him without words that his advances weren't welcome.

And yet she hadn't stopped him! Was there hope? Dared he go on? If he persisted would she unfreeze? Or would he make things even more difficult between them? He didn't want to fall out with her; they were partners now, even though she was resisting taking an active part in the business. Just as she was resisting his advances.

Even as these thoughts were passing through his mind Joshua was deepening his kiss, urging her lips apart, and when he felt a faint response his arms tightened. He hadn't lost her! She might believe that she hated him but her body was telling a different story.

His triumph was short-lived, however. She suddenly jerked free. 'Get away from me!' she yelled, her eyes feverishly bright. 'Don't ever do that again or I'll make sure you regret it for the rest of your life.'

What a wildcat. Her anger excited him. 'You could have stopped me any time you liked,' he said smartly. 'But you didn't. Why was that? I wonder. Were you enjoying it? Was it only belatedly that you remembered who you were kissing? It was good for us once; why not again?'

'Because I'm not the same person,' she retorted. She was pressed as far back in her chair as possible, her fingers gripping the arms tightly. 'You threw me out, don't forget. If I have to work and live with you then so be it, but as for anything else it's out of the question.'

'I think you enjoyed my kiss,' he said calmly. 'You're simply afraid to admit it, even to yourself.' He was disappointed by her reaction, but at least he'd found out that she wasn't totally immune to him.

Leanne couldn't believe that she had almost submitted to Joshua's kiss. The merest touch of his lips had sent a whole riot of sensation racing through her. But it wasn't love. Never love again. Pure sexual excitement, that was what it was. He was as devastatingly attractive as when they had met. She had wanted to go to bed with him on that first occasion; no love involved, simply hormones working overtime. And she felt the same now.

'You've nothing to say?'

Leanne tossed him a glance of disdain. 'It would be humanly impossible for me to enjoy your kisses. You seem to have a very high opinion of yourself.'

His smile was crooked and devastating. 'Maybe I have, or maybe it's that I know you better than you think.'

'Huh!' snorted Leanne. 'I doubt that very much.' If he had been in tune with her he would have known she couldn't possibly have had an affair with his brother. The truth was he didn't know her at all.

They were saved any further conversation by Courtney wandering out onto the veranda. She looked sweet in her nightie with her blonde hair tousled, her eyes tired and her thumb in her mouth.

'What's the matter, sweetheart?' she asked, grateful

that her little sister hadn't put in an appearance a minute or two earlier.

'I can't sleep. I dreamed about Mummy. I want Mummy.' Tears filled her eyes and Leanne gathered her up onto her lap.

'Mummy's in heaven, sweetheart, with Daddy. But they still love you lots, you know that. They'll love you forever more and they want you to be a good girl for me.'

'I'll be good,' she whispered. 'If I go back to bed, will you and Josh come and read me a story?'

'Of course we will.' Leanne glanced at Joshua, who nodded.

'Josh, you carry me,' said the little girl, visibly brightening. 'A piggyback.'

'I'll get her a drink of milk,' said Leanne, and when she joined them Joshua was lying on the bed at the girl's side and Courtney was gazing into his face as he told her a story.

He would make a wonderful father, thought Leanne grudgingly. They had talked about having children but, as they'd both wanted to enjoy a few years on their own first, it had never happened. And after their break-up she'd been thankful. She had never thought it fair on children when their parents split up. Poor Courtney was going through hell, far too young to really understand what had happened.

She sat on the corner of the bed watching her little sister as her eyes gradually closed. But Joshua went on with his tale about a naughty dragon until they were both sure that she was fast asleep.

'You're so good with her,' said Leanne as they tiptoed out of the room.

'She's a lovely kid.'

'She misses her parents so much.'

'As I expect you do,' he said softly. 'I'd sort of got used to my father not being around but you've always had your mum. It's been a double whammy for you.'

'You sound as though you feel sorry for me.'

He gave one of his slow, twisted smiles. 'I think you'll make it.'

'With no thanks to you,' she retorted. 'I can do without you forcing yourself on me. It was in very bad taste. That part of our lives is over.'

'And of course you have another man in your life,' he derided. 'I must confess that I would never have thought Ivan Eldridge your type. He's too rough, too much of the country boy.'

Maybe he was country but his heart was in the right place, and he'd always been polite and friendly towards her. And perhaps he did fancy her; he'd never said, because he knew that she didn't think of him in the same way, but he did look at her warmly sometimes, though she tried not to notice it.

But Josh had no right casting aspersions. 'How dare you? I'll choose whom I like to be my friend. I've known Ivan most of my life.' And she was so annoyed with him that she diverted sharply to her bedroom even though it was still early.

Not that she felt like sleeping. She showered and pulled on a light cotton T-shirt, then sat in a chair with her knees up to her chin and her arms around them. All was still and silent save for a chorus of frogs somewhere near the pool. She really ought to pull out the stops and clean it, thought Leanne, or she'd have it overrun by nature.

A shadow passed her window. Joshua! There were muslin curtains for privacy at all the windows and she hadn't switched on the light, but she felt sure he was hoping to catch sight of her. The window was tightly closed, the air-conditioning keeping the room pleasantly cool, but even as she watched he walked past again, and this time he paused.

Swift annoyance surged, and she sprang up and wrenched open the window. 'What the hell are you doing peering into my room?' And then saw that he had his back to her.

'I wasn't even aware I was outside your room,' he answered calmly. 'I heard a sound in the garden.'

'Frogs,' she answered caustically, feeling foolish.

'Really?'

'Yes, really. They're invading the pool.'

'I see. Then I won't disturb you any longer. Goodnight.'

Leanne began to close the window, but all of a sudden his hand came out to stop it and, pushing the curtain to one side, he leaned in, then, hooking his other hand around the back of her head, he kissed her. It all happened so swiftly she couldn't stop him. The threat she had issued earlier was forgotten as a desperate need bubbled to the surface and she kissed him back hard.

The need lasted all of five seconds, and then it was gone as the cold horror of the situation hit her. What was she doing? She was kissing the enemy, that was what. She was making a tragic mistake. She was sending out all the wrong signals. Escape wasn't possible, though. Joshua's hand held her head steady, committed her to him. 'Let me go!' she gritted against his mouth. *'Let me go!'*

Slowly he did so, but he was smiling. 'An instant response this time. It looks as if I'm on a winning streak.' And then he was gone before she could think of a suitably cutting reply.

What she wanted to know was why he felt the need to strike up some sort of a relationship. Or was it simply that she was the only available female in the area and his hormones were working overtime? Whatever, she could do without it.

She was so angry with herself now that she couldn't sleep and when Courtney cried out she was in her room in an instant. 'It's all right, sweetheart,' she said reassuringly. 'You were dreaming again. I'll climb into bed with you, shall I?'

Her sister gave a pleased nod and Leanne cuddled up to her. Whether it was the comfort of another presence she didn't know, but sleep soon claimed her and she didn't wake until after six, when she heard Joshua softly calling her name.

She opened her eyes and saw him standing over the bed and was about to give him a piece of her mind when he said, 'I'm sorry to disturb you but I had a call from Mark. He's now a proud father and I'm going over to England to hold the fort while he takes a couple of weeks off. I did promise I'd do it. Is Courtney all right?' He looked anxiously at the sleeping girl.

'She was dreaming again. It happens often. Pass my congratulations on to Mark and Sandra. Have you managed to get a flight?'

'I was lucky, a cancellation—if I can get to the

airport in time.' He shot a look at his watch and whirled for the door. 'I've a taxi waiting outside. I'll ring you.'

She was about to say there was no need but he had already gone.

It was such a relief. She got up and walked around the house and she fancied that she could breathe more easily. With a bit of luck, she thought, he would realise how much he was missing London and not come back.

And yet strangely she missed him. The days were empty without Joshua. It was the first time she had been really alone since the fire which had taken her mother and Steve. Thank goodness for Courtney or she would have gone truly mad.

Even her sister noticed the difference, young though she was. And if she asked once in a day when her big brother was coming back she asked a dozen times. 'I miss him,' she complained constantly. 'He tells me funny stories. He makes me laugh.'

Ivan too asked when she was expecting him. 'I've no idea,' answered Leanne. 'It could be tomorrow, it could be never.'

'Never?'

Leanne shrugged. 'Who knows? He has a business in London; he might want to stay there.'

'But he was taking such a keen interest in things here that I presumed this was where his life lay now. And with you, of course.'

Astonishment widened Leanne's eyes. 'Me? I don't think so. What we once felt for each other is dead and gone. I'd be happy if he didn't come back.'

'So would I,' said Ivan, but so quietly that Leanne didn't hear him.

*   *   *

'I have a confession to make.'

Joshua looked at his brother, dark brows lifted expectantly. He'd been in London for ten days now and was itching to get back to the vineyard. He would never have believed that his life could change so completely in such a short space of time. He felt stifled in his London apartment; he hated looking out of the window at nothing but rooftops. He craved the wide-open spaces of Australia.

'It's to do with Leanne.'

Joshua felt a pang of unease. Not more revelations. Not more damning evidence that she had betrayed their marriage. Not now that he'd discovered he was still in love with her.

'I lied.'

Joshua had been invited to dinner, and it had been rudely disturbed when young Master Gideon Powers decided to air his lungs. Sandra had immediately rushed up to him, and the two brothers were sipping a fine Bordeaux as they faced each other across the table.

'What do you mean, you lied?' asked Joshua, frowning deeply.

Mark cleared his throat and it was easy to see how difficult it was for him to speak. 'She didn't come on to me; it was the other way round. I constantly pestered her but she just as consistently rejected me. I was peeved and hurt and humiliated. And when she threatened to tell you I knew I had to get in first.'

Joshua felt as though he'd been punched in the solar plexus. He found it difficult to take in what Mark was telling him. He had believed his brother above Leanne. He had divorced her because he had taken Mark's word against hers. Mark, who had stolen so many of his girlfriends in the past. Mark the womaniser. How could he have been so blind, so stupid?

He thumped his fists on the table, a flush of rage colouring his face. 'Tell me I'm not hearing this.'

'I wish I could,' said Mark uneasily. 'And if I could undo what I've done then I would.'

'Dammit, you've ruined my life,' Joshua roared, pushing his chair back and leaping to his feet. 'Do you realise that?'

'It's not too late.'

'Yes, it is. Leanne doesn't love me any more—she hates my guts. And at this moment in time I hate yours, you lying swine.' He circled the table to stand above Mark. 'If it wasn't for your wife and child upstairs I'd knock the living daylights out of you.'

Mark moved unhappily. 'I deserve it.'

'You can bet you do. Why did you do it? *Why?*'

'Because I've always come second to you.' Mark pushed himself up and faced his older brother. 'You've no idea what it's been like living in your shadow. Father always loved you more than me; it was always you he asked to do things. And you always got the best girls. Taking them off you was the only way I could think of getting back at you. And most times it worked.'

'But to try and take my wife!' declared Joshua. 'What sort of an underhand trick was that? How low can you get?'

'I'm truly sorry,' said Mark. 'She was in fact the

only girl who never responded to me. She really loves you.'

'*Did!*' roared Joshua. 'Past tense.'

'I'm sure there's hope.'

'You think so? After the way I treated her?' Joshua ran an angry hand through his hair, his eyes blazing with a passion that consumed his whole body. 'God, I thought I could believe my own brother rather than someone I'd known for less than twelve months. I have to get out of here. Tell Sandra whatever you like but don't expect to see me again for a very long time.'

Once outside he dragged in huge breaths of air. Mark's confession had stunned him. He'd never known that Mark felt he'd come second in everything, and he was truly sorry if that was the case, but even so it didn't give him the right to tell lies, and such convincing ones at that.

He felt like battering his head against the wall. What was he to do? Could he possibly make it up to Leanne? Would she ever forgive him for doubting her? He didn't think so. And then he began to turn the blame on her. Why hadn't she stuck up for herself? Why hadn't she made him listen? Why hadn't she insisted that she was speaking the truth?'

Because she had. She had tried to tell him, but he'd been so incensed he wouldn't listen, wouldn't believe her. It had happened to him once before. Mark hadn't been involved on that occasion but he'd caught his girlfriend in the arms of another man, and when she'd sworn there was nothing in it, that it was just an old friend she'd bumped in to, he had believed her. Until it happened again. He had sworn then that he would never be taken for a fool a second time.

But he had been. He was the world's biggest fool.
And because of it he had lost the one woman he truly
loved. He hadn't realised that he still loved her; in
fact he'd been relieved when she left the country,
couldn't wait to divorce her, and in the intervening
years, after the initial heartache, he had tried not to
think of her. It was not until he'd gone over to
Australia for his father's funeral and come face to
face with her that the knowledge hit him with the full
force of a mighty hurricane.

His breathing was thick and heavy as he slowly
made his way to his apartment. He felt sick to the
very pit of his stomach. He'd meant it about wanting
to punch his brother. He wanted to kill him! Lord,
how could Mark have done such a thing, and kept it
a secret all these years? How could he live with himself? And what had made him confess now?

Joshua sat up all night, going over and over in his
mind everything that had been said between him and
Leanne. What a bastard he'd been, refusing to listen
to her pleas of innocence. He deserved to be whipped.

By morning he had reached a decision. He was
going to apologise profusely and plead with Leanne.
Get down on his knees if necessary. Perhaps she
could learn to love him again. He didn't deserve it,
he knew that, but he had to try. His one faint hope
was her ready response when he had kissed her
through the bedroom window.

He didn't know why he had done that after the way
she had yelled at him earlier. She had even threatened
him. And yet still he had kissed her. So maybe, a
very faint maybe, there was hope.

Before he left he made one very short, terse phone

call to Mark, telling him that he was leaving the country and that he'd better get back to work pronto.

During the flight he tried to work out what to say to Leanne. It seemed a futile exercise when he knew that she would tell him in no uncertain terms to get lost. But faint-hearted wasn't part of his make-up. He would persist for however long it took. He would wear down her resistance and one day she would learn to love him again. One day they would remarry. He had to hang on to that thought.

At the airport Joshua hired a car and broke every speed limit in his haste to be with her. He parked as near as he could to the house and leapt up the veranda steps. At first glance the house appeared to be empty, but then he saw her—coming out of the bedroom with Ivan Eldridge.

CHAPTER FIVE

LEANNE came to a sudden halt when she saw Joshua. She hadn't expected him back; not this soon anyway, if at all. She'd hoped he would come to understand that the two of them living together wasn't a good idea. She'd hoped that he would realise he loved his work in London more than he did wine-making.

Clearly they were futile hopes. He was here as large as life and contrarily she felt an instant buzz of awareness. Damn the man. She didn't want this to happen any more. He was out of her life; why the hell couldn't he stay out? The trouble was they'd had such a good sex life that simply looking at his magnificent body set her on fire.

It had all begun with that kiss. Up until then she had thought every loving ember dead. It had taken a long time to finally decide that he meant nothing to her. In the beginning it had been anger and hurt that she felt, such anger, so deep that she thought it would kill her. But gradually cold, hard emotions had taken its place. It was as though her heart was packed in ice, every vein frozen, and no man would be able to melt it ever again.

But one man had. The very man who had caused her body to shut down. And he was here now, facing her. She saw the smile in Joshua's eyes, the smile that had always made her race into his arms, a special smile reserved for her alone, one that told her she was very dear to him.

Now his smile faded, replaced first of all by shock, and secondly by cold accusation, his mouth turning grim—a mouth that knew every intimate part of her body. The very thought had her squeezing her thighs together in an effort to shut out these itinerant feelings.

Luck was on her side. Clearly Joshua thought she had been to bed with Ivan. An excellent excuse to maintain the fiction. In fact he couldn't have timed his return any better. She gave Ivan a brilliant smile before expressing her surprise at seeing Joshua. 'You should have let me know when you were coming.'

'So I see,' came his curt response.

She walked slowly towards him, Ivan tagging along at her side. 'How are Sandra and Mark?'

'Good,' he grunted, still eyeing her with a death-defying glare.

'And the baby?'

'What?' His eyes had turned to Ivan, coldly assessing, as if trying to work out what this man had that made Leanne want him.

'The baby. How is he?'

He swivelled his attention back to her. 'Like any other baby. Sleeping, crying, feeding. It's a never-ending cycle.'

'And Mark's gone back to work?'

'I hope so,' he grunted.

Leanne wondered what that meant but didn't feel she dared ask.

'I guess I ought to be getting back to work myself,' Ivan said, very aware of the tension between them.

He probably thought they needed to talk, thought Leanne, but did they hell. She had nothing to say to Joshua Powers. It was vital that she put as much distance between them as possible. She didn't want the third degree, not now, not any time.

Courtney once again came to the rescue. 'Josh! I didn't know you were here.' And she threw herself into his arms. Much as she herself had always done, thought Leanne bitterly. She hoped he never hurt the child as much as he had hurt her.

While Courtney chattered to Joshua she went outside with Ivan. 'Joshua doesn't look too happy,' he said.

'Jet lag,' she returned dismissively. 'It can be a killer if you don't stop over. And, knowing Joshua, he wouldn't do that; he'd be in too much of a rush. He's a workaholic, did you know? Oh, and thank you for fixing that hinge.'

He smiled warmly. 'Any time. And by the way, it really isn't necessary for him to bother with the paperwork. There's plenty for him to learn besides that.'

'Don't fret about it; it's the way he is,' she said airily. Out of the corner of her eye she saw Joshua come out onto the veranda with Courtney sitting on his shoulders, and perversely, because she knew exactly why he was there, she stood on tiptoe and gave Ivan a kiss. It was on the cheek actually but she knew that from Joshua's angle it would look as though she was kissing his mouth.

He looked surprised, and then pleased. 'Is this a hint that you're warming towards me?'

'Maybe I am,' she replied. Especially if it would stop Joshua trying to kiss her again. She knew what would happen if he did. It wouldn't be long before she was in bed with him. She wouldn't be able to help herself. And sex for the sake of it wasn't on her agenda.

'Shall we go out for a meal tonight?'

'I'd love to.' And Joshua could stay in and look after Courtney. The thought gave her surprising pleasure. In any case, she excused, after his long flight he would probably be glad of an early night.

She watched Ivan climb into his ute but not until he had driven out of the yard did she turn back towards the house. Joshua was still watching her, a warning light in his eyes.

Courtney jiggled excitedly. 'Josh is back.'

'He certainly is, sweetheart.'

'He's going to play with me.'

Joshua lifted her down. 'After I've had a few words with Leanne. Run along, there's a good girl.'

Courtney pouted, hesitated a moment, and then trotted obediently into the house. 'Was that necessary?' asked Leanne sharply. 'She's so pleased to see you. Your name hasn't been off her lips all the time you've been away.'

'But apparently not yours,' he growled. 'You've soon consoled yourself.'

'Consoled?' she yelped. 'What the devil's that supposed to mean? I have no reason to console myself. I was glad when you went.'

Eyes that she had gazed into and trembled at so many times, eyes that had sucked her into his very soul, looked coldly into hers. That they had once been one seemed inconceivable at this moment in time.

'How often does he come to the house?'

'Who?' He had no right asking these questions.

'Ivan the Terrible.'

'Only if we need each other.' The way she had needed him now to mend her hinge, or he needed her to go over some paperwork. But Joshua wouldn't know she meant that. Already she could see red anger flashing at the backs of his eyes.

'As you needed him this morning?' he asked icily. 'Or did he spend the night?'

Had he really thought she would stay in bed until after ten? She was always up with the birds. Although she could remember the days when she and Joshua had lazed a morning away in bed. Sundays, as a rule. Nothing to get up for and only each other to please. Sex had never been so good as in those early days of their marriage. Sometimes he had been gentle with her, sometimes their passion had run away with them. Exquisite thrill had followed exquisite thrill. And, sated, they had lain in each other's arms for hours.

'I don't think I need answer that question,' she retorted, equally coldly.

Blue ice glittered between half-closed lids. 'Because the truth's glaringly obvious?'

'Because you'll believe only what you want to believe,' she snapped. 'Like always. This is a pointless conversation.'

For just a second his jaw tightened grimly. 'Maybe I'll go and ask Ivan a few questions.'

Leanne allowed one eyebrow to rise. 'You think he'd tell you what's going on in our private life?' Mentally she crossed her fingers that Joshua wouldn't speak to Ivan; she didn't want her friend inadvertently letting her down—she wanted to carry on the illusion.

'He might. He might be proud of it, willing to talk about you.'

'To my ex-husband? I don't think so,' she flared. 'And by the way, I'm eating out with him tonight.'

Eyes narrowed yet again. 'And Courtney? What's happening to her?' he asked sharply. But she knew that Courtney wasn't the real issue.

'I'll ask Molly to babysit.'

'She's used to doing that, is she?' he asked accusingly.

'Actually no. I've never left her.'

'And you're not going to leave Courtney to a stranger now,' he barked. 'I'll look after her.'

Leanne felt a smile of satisfaction spread through her.

Joshua strode away from Leanne with all the fires of hell burning inside him. He'd had such high hopes. On the never-ending flight he'd gone over and over in his mind what he would say to her. Even when he'd slept he'd dreamt about their reunion, about the tender sweetness of it. And now everything lay in ruins.

He'd known it would be a long haul, but what he hadn't expected was to fight off another man as well. Ivan wasn't for her, he knew that even if Leanne didn't. He was a bullish man with no finesse and Joshua also had his suspicions about his trustworthiness. But that was something he was keeping to himself until he had proof.

He threw his case down on the bed, ripped his clothes off, and let the fierce jets of the shower beat down on his anguished body. He had so wanted to apologise to Leanne, to tell her that Mark had come up with the truth at last, and ask if she could ever forgive him for doubting her.

Instead he was still her number-one enemy and she was seeing another man. Damn! He bounced his fists off the tiled wall, pressed his forehead against it and with the water beating down on his back he stood there for ages, breathing deeply, until finally he had himself under control.

Roughly he towelled himself dry, dragging on a fresh set of clothes from his wardrobe, tossing the contents of his case into the laundry basket. When he emerged from his room Courtney was hovering. Lord, he'd forgotten that he'd promised to play with her. And he needed to get out of the house while he sorted his thoughts and decided on his next course of action.

'Run and tell Leanne we're going for a walk.'

'Leanne's gone.'

'Gone?' he asked with a frown. 'Where?'

'To make wine.'

To be with Ivan! His gut tightened. 'Then we'll join her,' he said with an attempt at enthusiasm. But all the way down to the winery he was fuming.

Joshua knew that he had no control over what his ex-wife did, but to see her making a mistake with the likes of Ivan Eldridge was not something he intended to ignore.

He found her in the office with him. They were poring over some paperwork on the desk but Ivan was standing much closer to Leanne than was necessary. There was less than a hair's breadth between them, and Leanne looked at Joshua crossly as he stalked into the room.

'I didn't expect to see you here yet,' she said, sounding defensive.

'Is that why you left Courtney behind?'

'She wanted to be with you.'

'I found her lurking outside my door. If I'd gone to bed then what the hell would have happened to her? You're being totally irresponsible. How much of this has been going on while I've been away?'

'It hasn't,' she retorted, her beautiful green eyes flashing magnificently. 'You know I'd never leave Courtney on her own, would I, sweetheart?' She looked at her baby sister for confirmation.

But Courtney wasn't listening; she was too busy running circles around Joshua's legs. And he was thinking how beautiful Leanne was and what a fool he had been to let her go. Every fibre of his being was alerted to her, and he wanted to snatch her away from Ivan's side and carry her up to the house to make love.

And when they had finished, when she was soft and pliant in his arms, when they were as close in both body and mind as two people could be, then he would convince her that Ivan wasn't the right man. She would listen once she had fallen under his spell again.

It had been so good for them in the beginning. Love at first sight on both sides. When he had seen her at the party he had known instantly that she was the girl he wanted to spend the rest of his life with. It had never happened to him before. He had admired girls, yes, he had fancied them, he had taken them to bed, but there had never been that instant recognition of a life partner. And he had blown it.

He hated himself for letting her down, in fact he knew that he would never forgive himself, ever. If, and it looked like being a big if, he ever managed to persuade her to try again then he would spend the rest of his life making it up to her.

But that was all in the future; it was the now, this precise moment in time, that was of paramount importance. He had to separate them. 'Courtney needs you,' he said, 'because I'm going to drag Ivan away.'

Leanne looked as though she was about to refuse, about to tell him that he could take care of his sister himself, but after a quick, apologetic glance at Ivan she nodded. 'Come on, Courtney,' she said, holding out her hand, 'let's go back to the house.'

'No!' Brown eyes sparked defiance. 'I want Josh.' And she stamped her tiny foot.

Joshua grinned and squatted down beside her. 'I'll be back soon, I promise, and then we can play for as long as you like.'

'Play with my dolls?'

Joshua squirmed inside but he kept his face deadly serious. 'Of course. And you can get them ready while you're waiting. What shall we play? Shall we pretend we're taking them to the park?'

'Yes,' said Courtney excitedly. 'And play ball as well.'

This was much more in his line. 'Play ball,' he agreed.

And so Leanne took Courtney away and Joshua spent the next two hours in Ivan's company. And the more he saw of the guy the more convinced he became that Leanne was making the biggest mistake of her life.

'Leanne tells me you're taking her out this evening.' It was the end of the morning and he was ready to go up to the homestead for lunch. 'Is it something you do often?' He saw the wariness that entered Ivan's eyes, his faintly shifty expression.

The big man shrugged. 'Now and then. She's lonely.'

And Ivan thought jumping into her bed would help. He saw her as an easy target. He was taking advantage, in fact. Joshua would like to bet that he hadn't tried anything on while their parents were alive. 'Not any longer.' He couldn't help himself; he had to say it.

'Are you suggesting that there's a chance of you getting back together?' asked Ivan with a frown.

'Every chance.'

'She's said nothing to me.'

'Why should she?' he asked with a lift of his well-shaped brows.

'Well, she—'

'Doesn't have to tell you everything. I wouldn't be surprised if she didn't cancel your date this evening now that I'm home.'

'No, she won't,' said Ivan quickly. 'Leanne won't let me down, I'm confident of that.'

And Joshua knew he was right. But he wasn't going to let Ivan know it. Let him think that he didn't stand much of a chance now that her ex was back on the scene.

When she saw Joshua striding towards the house Leanne groaned. She had hoped, in fact she had prayed that he would stay away. Courtney was asleep and she didn't want to spend time alone with him. He would challenge her about Ivan again, of that she was very sure, and she needed Ivan. He was her protection against this man who had ruined her life once and was trying to do the same again.

'What are you doing back?' she demanded as he strode into the kitchen.

'I promised Courtney.'

'She's having her midday nap.'

'That's good, because you and I need to talk again.'

'If it's about Ivan then forget it,' she snapped.

His brows arched into two question marks. 'Touchy about him, are we?'

'I just don't want you poking your nose in where it's not wanted,' she retorted hotly. 'I've known Ivan a lot longer than I've known you. We understand each other perfectly.'

'Maybe it's not Ivan I want to talk about.'

She froze for a second. 'Then what is it?' Not themselves, not the kiss they had exchanged before he left? Surely he wasn't hoping that it had meant something to her; that there was a chance of a reconciliation? Because there wasn't. Not a cat in hell's.

'Let me get washed up and we'll talk over a leisurely lunch.'

Usually he couldn't be bothered; he'd grab a quick bite and then go back to work double quick. So what exactly did he have in mind? Her mind raced as she made a jug of chilled juice and set it out on the kitchen table. It was much too hot to sit outside. The temperature was baking; she couldn't even remember the last time they'd had rain.

She'd already made sandwiches and she put those

out too, together with an apple pie she'd baked yesterday. By the time she had finished Joshua was back and he sat down and grabbed a sandwich as though he was starving.

'I've missed this place,' he said, leaning back on the wooden kitchen chair, stretching his long, muscular legs out in front of him, looking around with a sense of satisfaction.

It was a big, farmhouse-type kitchen with a range and a scrubbed wooden table and onions hanging from a hook in the ceiling. Artificial ones but realistic all the same. There were storage shelves rather than cupboards, which meant that everything had to be kept very tidy. Leanne loved it. She loved anything with character.

Joshua's kitchen in his London apartment was stainless-steel slick. Smart, modern, easy to keep clean, but without a soul. Give her this one any time. And it looked as though he felt the same way, she realised uneasily.

He looked as relaxed as she had ever seen him, munching on his cheese and ham sandwich, giving no indication that their conversation would be anything other than pleasant.

And as she looked at him Leanne couldn't help but be stirred by the sight of his big, sexy body. So many good times they had had. Her pulses leapt erratically at the very thought. And she closed her eyes so that she wouldn't see him, but it made no difference because the memories were still there.

More than once they'd made love in the stainless-steel kitchen. He would creep up behind her and she'd feel his urgent need, and before she knew it her skirt would ride high, her panties would drop, and he'd enter her with swift expertise. She had loved it when he took her unexpectedly like that.

And she couldn't help wondering now what it would be like to make love in this beautiful, homely kitchen. And yes, it was homely; very much so. It was no wonder he was so relaxed.

'What are you thinking?'

Her eyes snapped open, the pulse at her throat throbbed and her throat itself tightened. She looked at him in something akin to panic. He'd been watching her! What had her face given away?

'Why do you ask?'

'You were miles away. Back in England, perhaps?'

Oh, lord, he knew.

'Or was it Ivan?'

Faint relief.

'Why don't you eat?'

'Because I'm not hungry.'

'Saving room for your meal tonight, is that it?'

'I'm looking forward to it, yes.' At least it would get her away from Joshua. It would give her the breathing space that she needed. Breathing space? Goodness! He'd only been back a few hours. What was the matter with her?

'I'd rather you didn't go.'

'Because you don't like him? Because you don't think he's good enough for me? Don't start that again, Josh.'

'How can you compare him to what we once had?' he demanded. 'Don't you remember how good it was between us? Do you feel that with Ivan? No, you bloody well don't.' He threw his sandwich on the table and stood up; and the next second he hauled her to her feet and kissed her.

'Do you feel this with Ivan? And this? And this?' His kisses were everywhere, his hands everywhere. He was awakening every feeling she had long thought dead.

CHAPTER SIX

LEANNE wanted Joshua to stop kissing her. She wanted to be anywhere but here with him assaulting her senses. It made a mockery of every vow she had taken since their break-up. He was inflicting himself on her and he was expecting a response, expecting something more than the icy stillness she maintained.

It was that earlier kiss that had done it. She ought never to have let him see that he still had the power to stir her. He was using it to his advantage now and there was little or nothing she could do to stop the flow.

'Don't try to ignore what I know you're feeling inside,' he growled against her mouth. 'You're fooling no one.'

His kisses became more hot and urgent and his thumb and forefinger, tweaking her nipple in exactly the way he knew would arouse her, combined to make her blood run like liquid silver through her veins. She felt boneless. She felt that if he let her go she would collapse into a molten puddle on the floor.

And in the end she could hold back no longer. Her whole body leapt in response. She pressed herself against him, thigh against thigh, hip against hip, feeling the full, exciting power of his arousal.

His reaction was to slide both his hands down either side of her body, slowly, tantalisingly, feeling every hot inch of her, until they cupped her bottom and urged her even harder into him.

She wanted to wind her legs around him the way she had in the past; she wanted him to lay her back on the table and slide himself into her; she wanted to experience once again the heart-thumping excitement that only he was capable of giving her.

In short, she wanted him.

The realisation hit with the might of a force-ten gale. And yet, rather than feeling horrified, she wanted him to go on. It was a case of once started, she couldn't stop. She curled her fingers into his hair, pulling his head close, opening her mouth readily to his kisses. She heard the moans of hunger emanating from her throat, a reflex reaction because this deeply sensuous man was drawing every atom of sizzling sensation from her.

She wanted to rip off all their clothes, she wanted to feel him, to look at him, to enjoy what she had once had with him. Not the love part, never the love part again, but the great sex. He made her feel alive, all woman, feminine woman, powerful woman, capable of inciting him too.

And almost as though he heard her thoughts he began undressing her, and in trembling excitement she did the same to him. As buttons were undone on her blouse, so did they pop open on his shirt. And as the zip on her shorts slid down, so did his. It was a game of copycat. An entirely new game, and, judging by the glittering intensity in his eyes, he was relishing it.

Not until they were completely disrobed and she could feast her eager eyes on his strongly muscled body did doubts begin to enter Leanne's mind. And even then they were fleeting ones. He was utterly magnificent—maybe a little heavier than five years ago, but he still had a fine physique; still had a flat stomach and powerful leg muscles. The other, more intimate part of his anatomy was exactly as she remembered and her eyes were drawn to this tantalising part of him time and time again.

'Like what you see, do you?' he asked gruffly, pulling her hard against him.

'Mmm.' It was a grudging acknowledgement.

'And I like what I see. Very much.' He traced his hands gently over her face, touching her eyebrows and her eyelids; her high cheekbones and her nose. When he traced the outline of her lips she sucked his finger into her mouth, nibbling it with her even white teeth, stroking it with her tongue, feeling a sense of power when he writhed uncontrollably against her.

'You little minx,' he breathed harshly. 'You'll pay for that.'

He lifted her into his arms and, heedless of their nakedness, he carried her through to his bedroom. Something in the back of her mind told her that he was doing this in case Courtney woke and walked in on them. And all the time he was kissing her—probably to stop her protesting. Not that she would have done. She was far too excited, far too ready.

Josh's lovemaking was all and more than she remembered. He took her to the heights and back again. At first it was animal passion but after that his lovemaking became gentle and considerate and Leanne lay there long after it was over, simply marvelling that it could still be as good despite all that had happened between them.

It wasn't until she slowly came back down to earth that cold reality set in. And with it self-disgust. How could she have been so stupid as to let this happen? She bounced off the bed and glared at him. 'If you think this has made any difference to how I feel about you you're mistaken. It was sex, that's all.'

He pushed himself up on one elbow, looking completely unperturbed. He nodded slowly and thoughtfully. 'Good sex.'

His ever-present whimsical smile made her even angrier. 'Good, bad or indifferent, it doesn't matter.'

'But you'd do it again?'

'Not on your life,' she yelled.

'So what made you do it now?'

She had no answer. What *had* made her do it? Heaven alone knew. It was her body taking over. Not her heart, not her head, just her body. It had craved to be made love to. No one had done it since Joshua. *No one could do it like Joshua!* Damn! She didn't want to think that, even though she suspected it might be true. And she was lying. She *would* do it again.

She'd had a taste of what she'd been missing. And what a sweet taste. It was like honey, like nectar, the elixir of life. Her whole body still felt alive and glowing. She wanted more. Dared she do it? Could she carry on a loveless affair?

Angry with herself now, she swung around and ran through to the kitchen, where she swept up her clothes and took them to the bathroom. With the door safely closed behind her she was able to breathe more easily.

But no less painfully. Had she created a precedent? Would he demand more? Would he take advantage?

So many questions whirled in her mind as she stepped into the shower, none of which she could answer. She kept her eyes tightly closed, and tried to shut Joshua out too. What an impossible feat. He surrounded her. His presence was ever-powerful. She even fancied that he was in the bathroom with her. He was taking over the whole house. Why had she let him live with her? Why hadn't she insisted that he find himself lodgings?

And all of a sudden he *was* there, his hands were touching her, his body sliding erotically against hers. Tell me this isn't happening, she pleaded with herself. Tell me I'm dreaming. But she had no such luck.

She snapped open her eyes and he stood beside her, larger than life. He was smiling...even his eyes were smiling; there was nothing she could take offence to, except his presence! And how could she ban him after the way she had virtually thrown herself at him? She was in a stalemate situation.

'I don't want you here.' Her liquid green eyes looked uncertainly into his.

'I'm saving water.'

It wasn't funny. 'You have no right.'

'You didn't fight me off earlier.'

'I was a fool.'

'A beautiful one.'

'And I'm getting out of here. Feel free to carry on by yourself.' All she wanted was to leap back into her clothes. She needed protection. For her own peace of mind she needed to form some sort of barrier between them. Ideally it would be a door and a lock and a bolt. But if a shirt and shorts were all she had then so be it.

His smile changed to a wicked grin as he let her go; and never had Leanne dressed so quickly. She gave herself a quick dab with the towel, tugged on her gear and sped out of the room.

She went into the kitchen and began tossing plates and cutlery into the dishwasher, all the time her mind working furiously. She was angry with herself for letting her feelings get the better of her. Sex had never formed a big part of her life, so why now? The answer was glaringly obvious. She had never met another man who stirred her senses to such a degree.

This whole wine-sharing thing was going to be a huge disaster. Rather than bringing them together it would force them apart. She craved his body but she didn't love him as a man. How stupid was that?

And tonight she had to go out with Ivan! The very thought made her feel sick. How could she hide from him what had happened between her and Joshua? It would be emblazoned on her forehead for everyone to see.

Even now, even though she was fuming, she could still feel Joshua inside her. Her senses were still zinging. If he came into the kitchen she could quite easily sling a plate at him, but it didn't alter the fact that he was the cause of her feeling like this.

What was keeping them? Joshua had expected Leanne home long ago. When she'd admitted that she was still going out with Ivan he had at first disbelieved her and then been extremely angry.

'I don't believe it. I thought—oh , never mind what

I thought.' He had rubbed his hand over the back of his neck and glared at her. 'Go and have a good time. Forget that you were making love to me a few hours ago; don't even tell Ivan when you let him make love to you.'

A deep flush coloured her neck and cheeks. 'That's uncalled-for.'

'Is it?' he asked, raising his brows. 'If our love-making meant anything to you you'd have cancelled your date.'

'Precisely, and I haven't because it meant nothing. It was just sex. Enjoyable sex, admittedly, but that's all it was. I don't love you. That part of our life is over.'

'Do you love Ivan?' He prayed that she didn't because it would make his task so much harder. He wanted her to fall back in love with him. He would use everything in his power to make her do so. But if she loved another man...

'I don't think my feelings for Ivan should be part of this conversation.'

'But you let him make love to you?'

'That's none of your business either.'

'I damn well want to make it my business,' he hurled furiously. 'I don't want to see you getting hurt.'

Leanne's eyes flashed. 'That's rich, coming from you.'

She had such beautiful eyes, wide-spaced and a lovely sloe shape, and their colour changed constantly from the palest topaz to the richest emerald and all shades in between. They fascinated him. The first day they met, when they'd sat and talked and got to know each other, he hadn't been able to take his eyes off them. They had totally enchanted him.

And they still did. He could look at her forever, whether she was flashing them in anger as she was now, or whether they were soft and dewy when they were making love. They were so clear and full of passion. They were by far her best feature. Not that the rest of her fell far behind. She was perfect in every way and he constantly chastised himself for letting her go.

He had wanted to tell her then that he had made a mistake, that he should have believed her and not Mark, but it wasn't the right moment, not when she was about to get ready to go out with another man.

But all the time they were away he had been consumed with raging jealousy. He had tried to read, he had tried to watch TV, but nothing had worked. He'd ended up sitting out on the veranda waiting for her. And while he waited he had relived those magical moments.

He'd hardly been able to believe his luck when Leanne reacted so spectacularly to his kiss. It was his every dream come true, probably even better because of the intervening years. She was exactly the same uninhibited lover as she'd always been. He had even hoped, felt even, that this could be the beginning of a new life together.

When she'd declared that it meant nothing to her, that it was pure, unadulterated sex, he'd felt poleaxed. He could not believe that his one-time wife could behave like that towards him and then blithely deny any emotional involvement.

He'd have bet his last penny that Leanne wasn't

the type to enjoy sex for the sake of it. She'd always said that she believed in the power of love. What he'd adored about her were her quaint, old-fashioned ideas where love and romance were concerned. She didn't believe, she said, in all the free love that was floating around. She didn't believe in jumping into bed with a man you'd just met.

So what was she doing making love with him if it meant nothing to her?

And did she love Ivan?

He'd seen both of them come out of her bedroom, and they hadn't even had the decency to look guilty.

What was going on?

It was almost midnight. A canopy of stars glittered above like a diamond web. The frogs still croaked, an owl hooted, a distant horse whinnied, but there was still no sound of a car's engine. All respectable people were in bed.

He got up and paced the veranda, going around and around the house like a lost soul. He had switched off all the lights and every little sound had his ears pricking, but it was almost a quarter past the hour before he finally heard the faint purr of an approaching vehicle.

Resuming his seat, he waited. It took a few more minutes before it reached the homestead, gravel crunching beneath its tyres as it slowly drew closer, finally coming to a gentle halt. The big gum tree shielded him from the car's headlights and Joshua's nostrils flared as he took in a disapproving sniff.

As the door opened and the interior light came on he saw Leanne lean across and give Ivan a peck on the cheek. But Ivan wanted more. Ivan hooked a hand behind her head and kissed her full on the lips. And she didn't pull away.

Joshua felt an ache deep in his gut. He wanted to go across and smash the man's face, but caution prevailed. He couldn't help but wonder, though, whether the reason they were so late was that they had been back to Ivan's house, and this kiss was the finale to a passion-spent evening.

He felt a red haze blotting out his vision. Sitting here was doing him no good. He stumbled into the house before either of them saw him, and when Leanne finally came indoors he was already shut in his bedroom.

Deep breathing did no good, nor did telling himself that it was no business of his, and he knew that he would get no sleep if he didn't speak to Leanne and find out what had gone on. But would she thank him for it? Would he do more harm than good?

He guessed the answer to that but even so it took every ounce of self-control to stop himself from tramping into her room and demanding a blow-by-blow account of her evening. He didn't sleep, not a wink, and he knew that when morning came he would ask the same questions he wanted to ask now.

Never had a night seemed so long. When finally the purple shadows were chased away by the golden glow of a rising sun he ducked into his shower, pulled on a pair of white cotton trousers and a summer blue shirt, and headed for the kitchen.

Leanne was there before him. He was surprised because he hadn't heard any movement. She sat at the table, still in her nightie, a mug of coffee cradled in her palms, and he was able to observe her for a moment or two before she saw him. She looked tired, not in the least as though she'd had a thoroughly enjoyable evening and slept the sleep of the contented.

'You're up early,' she said, turning bleary eyes in his direction.

'And so are you. What sort of a time did you have that you couldn't sleep?' He oughtn't to have said that; he oughtn't to have made any reference to last night. At least not yet.

She was immediately on the defensive. 'Wonderful, actually. The food at Kidman's is superb.'

'And the company?' He still couldn't help himself.

'Excellent. We bumped into another couple that we knew and the time simply flew. It was almost midnight before we knew it.'

So they hadn't gone back to Ivan's place! The discovery brought a smile to Joshua's lips. 'I'm glad you enjoyed it. Is there any coffee?'

'It's instant, but the kettle's boiled. Help yourself.'

With his mug in his hand he sat down opposite Leanne. Simply looking at her made his heartbeat quicken, and the thought that she wore nothing beneath the nightshirt with its 'Good Morning Australia' motif was enough to send his testosterone levels sky-high.

'So what are your plans for today?' he asked. She looked as though she ought to go back to bed. In fact he'd like to take her. Not that she would sleep much then, but maybe afterwards...

'I'm taking Courtney into Tanunda. I have a dental appointment and she needs some new clothes.'

'I'll come with you,' he said instantly. He would enjoy that. They'd be like a family. He would be so proud to have Leanne at his side and little Courtney dancing around them.

'And miss out on your learning?' she scorned. 'Shame on you, Josh. I thought it was the most important thing in your life.'

You are the most important, he wanted to say. But he didn't. 'It is important to me, yes, but I could look after Courtney while you're at the dentist's. You know what a fidget she is.'

'I can manage, thank you,' she said. 'You carry on with what you're doing here. Ivan was saying how much knowledge you'd picked up already. He said you're like a sponge, soaking it all in as quickly as he gives it to you.'

Joshua wasn't sure whether that was a compliment or a complaint. Not that it mattered; he couldn't care less about the other man's opinion. 'Have you given any more thought to developing a programme? I'm honestly amazed that the company hasn't been properly computerised long before now. It must be falling far behind its competitors.'

'My father was a Luddite,' declared Leanne. 'He hated change.'

'But my father wasn't. Why didn't he alter things?'

'Because my mother wouldn't let him. I guess she thought it would be letting my father down in some way.'

'And do you feel the same?'

Leanne shrugged. 'I guess not. I haven't really given it much thought.'

'Then I think you should. I think it's important for the success of the company. If you won't do it I'll get an outsider in.'

'Which will cost.'

'I know that.'

'So it's ridiculous.'

'Then you do it.'

Leanne drew in a long, ragged breath and finally nodded. 'OK. I'll come down to the office when I get back and you can tell me exactly what it is you want. I'll need a computer here, of course, and we'll need new equipment down at the site.'

'Which is already on order,' he told her with a faintly wry smile.

'You did it without asking me?'

Joshua shrugged his wide shoulders. 'I knew you'd come round to it sooner or later.'

CHAPTER SEVEN

LEANNE wasn't looking forward to working closely with Joshua. It was her worst nightmare come true. It was bad enough that he was here, in Australia, living on her property, but normally she could avoid him for most of the day. Not now though. Goodness knew why he was so insistent that they upgrade their office system when it had always worked perfectly well.

It would be better for the company, she knew that. She'd even told her mother so on several occasions, but Pauline hadn't been interested. In truth her parent had only played at running the vineyard. It wasn't her first passion. Her mother had been a home-maker above all else, and she hadn't cared so long as it ran along smoothly and didn't cause her any problems. After Hugh died, and even after she'd remarried, she had left everything in Ivan's capable hands. And Steve had gone along in much the same mould as her father. Leanne didn't see why Joshua couldn't do it as well.

Admittedly he was used to upgrading business strategies, but this was different. He wasn't being paid to do it, and although he owned half of the company she owned the other half and should surely have a say. Instead he was taking over—and, fool that she was, she was letting him. And why? Because she didn't want to spend any more time with him than was strictly necessary, that was why.

Leanne had her lunch in town, not able to face the thought of eating at home with Joshua. She was still far too sensitive to his presence. When he'd come down for coffee early this morning she had wanted to suggest they go back to bed and make love. She craved his body! It was absolute insanity and yet she couldn't help herself.

If only she had never let him touch her. If only she had not responded to his advances. If… The trouble was she couldn't help it. It was as though she was programmed to do it. Her need of him had been set up on the day they met in England. It was her destiny.

When she'd gone out with Ivan she had promised herself that she would forget Joshua and concentrate on enjoying the evening. How impossible was that? Joshua loomed large in her brain, filling her mind's eye, refusing to go away.

She hadn't even wanted Ivan to touch her, and several times he'd asked her what was wrong. When she'd repeatedly denied that there was anything he'd said bitterly, 'It's Joshua, isn't it? He doesn't like you coming out with me. He's trying to drive a wedge between us. He wants to get rid of me and take over the business himself.'

'Why would he do that?'

'Because he's still in love with you.'

'Rubbish!' she had declared strongly. 'He wants to make money, that's what. Not content with one successful business at home, he wants to improve this one as well. He probably wants to compete with Orlando.'

'Orlando?' Ivan had sneered. 'They've been going for nearly a hundred and sixty years.'

'And their Jacob's Creek is known around the world. We both know that but it won't stop him. Joshua has very big ideas. It won't finish with a new computer system—he'll want to expand. He'll drive himself on and on until he's the biggest wine producer in Australia.' And she probably wasn't far off the mark. Joshua was a focused man. Whether it was in his business or his love life Joshua usually got what he wanted.

When Leanne got home she left Courtney with Molly and slowly made her way down to where she knew Joshua would be waiting. She half expected Ivan to be present also; indeed she hoped he was, but fortune didn't favour her.

Joshua was poring over the books when she walked into the office, a pad in front of him filled with hastily scribbled notes. He turned and smiled when he heard her soft footfalls. 'Ah, good, you're here. Let's get started.'

She wished he wouldn't smile like that. It did her no good at all. It set her hormones dancing, it made her body want to gravitate towards his, it made her... No! She wouldn't think along those lines. This was business. Keep it that way.

Impossible! Sitting close to Joshua while he explained what he wanted, feeling his thigh brush hers far more frequently than was necessary, listening to the sound of his voice, remembering how he used those deep tones to their full advantage when he was making love to her, filled her with confusion.

'Are you sure you've got that?'

Leanne snapped herself back to what they were doing. Concentration was out of the question. This man knew more about her than anyone else. They had been lovers first and husband and wife second. Now they were in danger of becoming lovers again.

How it had happened when he'd chucked her out of both his life and his home she didn't know. She felt sure he hadn't had a change of heart. Joshua wouldn't do that. He was simply seizing the opportunity. He was a hot-blooded male who needed sex. There was no way he could remain celibate. And as she was the only woman available...

So, knowing all this, why did she respond so readily? Because she needed sex as well. *No, she didn't.* If that was all she needed, why hadn't she had an affair with Ivan? Because Joshua was her burning need.

'Leanne?'

'I'm sorry, what did you say?' Lord, she must stop this.

'I think perhaps we've done enough for today.'

Thank goodness!

'I'll walk back to the house with you.' He stretched his arms above his head and arched his back, relaxing muscles that had sat stiff for too long. Beneath his thin blue shirt Leanne could see the power of his body, and she felt an insane urge to touch him, to feel those hard muscles beneath her fingertips.

Damn! She shook her head and pushed back her chair. She really must take hold of herself. This mustn't be allowed to go on.

'Where's Courtney?' he asked.

He'd broken the spell, thank goodness. 'At Molly's house.'

'I'll fetch her. You look done in. Go and take a

long shower. And when I get back I'm going to clean that pool. It's about time we made use of it.'

'You don't have to,' she said quickly. If anything had put her off doing it, it was the thought of swimming with Joshua. Being half naked with Joshua. Looking at his magnificent body. Joshua looking at her! Every single one of these thoughts sent a *frisson* of awareness through her.

'But I want to. Does Courtney swim?'

'Of course.' Her mother had taught her youngest daughter to swim almost before she could walk. She was like a little fish in the water. She would love being able to use the pool again. And Joshua would be good with her, she knew that. It was herself she didn't trust.

True to his word, Joshua scrubbed and vacuumed until the pool was sparkling and inviting. Leanne wasn't sure where he got all his energy from—it exhausted her simply watching him.

Courtney had wanted to help, getting in his way; laughing in delight when he good-naturedly chased her away. She went to bed much later than usual and even then she didn't want to go; she wanted to stop and play with her brother in the pool.

Joshua solved the problem by agreeing to read her an extra bedtime story, and promising they would swim as much as she liked tomorrow.

Did that mean he wasn't going to work? That he'd be around all day? The very thought sent a shiver of apprehension down Leanne's spine. It was a pity her computer hadn't arrived because then she could spend her time setting it up.

'Did you order me a desk and chair with the com-

puter?' she asked Joshua as they ate their supper after
Courtney was finally settled.

'Naturally. Everything you'll need, in fact. They
should arrive tomorrow.'

Despite her misgivings Leanne was looking forward to developing the programme. She loved looking after her sister but it wasn't the sort of life she
had envisaged for herself. She missed going out to
work.

'I'm going to change my mother's sewing room
into an office,' she told him. 'I'll keep the sewing
machine and table but everything else can go.' She
hadn't the same interest in dressmaking or craft that
her mother had had.

'Do you think you'll cope with Courtney demanding your attention every second minute?' he asked.
'Perhaps we should think about asking Molly to look
after her full-time.'

Leanne didn't like the idea but she also knew how
impossible it would be to get on with her work with
her young sibling hanging around. 'Short-term, perhaps,' she agreed. 'And only if Courtney's happy.'

'Maybe Molly could look after her here,' he said
thoughtfully, 'and then Courtney won't feel that
there's another upheaval going on in her life.'

Leanne nodded. 'I'll ask her later.'

But later never came. Quite how it happened
Leanne wasn't sure, but one minute they were sitting
on the veranda, and the next they were racing each
other in the pool.

She had no chance of beating him, she'd known
that before she started. On their honeymoon in
Barbados she'd swum with him, and even though she

was a strong swimmer he'd made her efforts look puny. He had such strength in his arms and legs that he powered through the water like a torpedo.

'I don't know why I try to race you,' she panted as she reached his side, 'when I know you'll always win.'

'Ah, but I'm out of practice. You had every opportunity. I intend taking full advantage of this pool from now on, and I hope you'll join me.'

As he spoke he looked at her trim body and Leanne turned away. There was smouldering desire in his eyes as they rested on the swell of her breasts above her black swimsuit. She'd toyed with the idea of wearing a bikini and decided it was too hazardous, yet this neat little swimmer was still showing too much for his feasting eyes.

They were like intense blue probes, filling her with heat and passion, and with a tiny cry she pushed herself off from the edge and began to swim back, concentrating on propelling herself through the water as hard as she could. It was the only way she could work off her excess emotions.

When she reached the other end he stood at the side of the pool, waiting for her. She hadn't even suspected he might do that, hadn't even looked to see where he was.

His smile told her that he knew exactly why she had swum away from him. It was a knowing smile, a deeply sensual smile; it melted her bones. He was such a gorgeous man, how could she deny herself him? What a stupid question. She couldn't deny him, that was the trouble.

'Trying to prove something?' he asked, holding out a hand.

Leanne hesitated before taking it. Electricity and water didn't mix. And when she did allow him to pull her up an instant zing shot through her body. She snatched away because she knew what would happen if she didn't.

His response was a slow, crooked smile. The sky above them was a deep midnight-blue—in fact it was midnight—but an almost full moon lit the terrace as brilliantly as if it were day. Joshua's skin gleamed like polished silver, his torso so tautly muscled and inviting that it was all she could do not to throw herself in his arms.

It was sheer hell him living here but it was too late now to suggest that he find lodgings elsewhere. She ought to have done it in the beginning, except that she hadn't realised then exactly how much he would destroy her peace of mind and disrupt her entire life.

For only one thing was she thankful to him, and that was being here after their respective parents had died. She could never have coped on her own. He had been her strength and her support and she would be eternally grateful—but she could do without him now.

She'd like to bet her last dollar that her mother, and Steve for that matter, when they made their wills had had no idea how difficult they would make life for her, or for both of them in fact.

Admittedly her mother had always cherished the hope that they'd get back together, but that wouldn't have been in her mind when she made her will. She would have hoped to live for another thirty years at least. All she'd wanted was for the business to remain in the family.

Were they looking down on them now, worrying about the problems they had caused; wishing they could change everything? Or were they hoping that the two of them would resolve their differences and get back together?

Leanne hadn't realised that she was shivering until Joshua deftly draped a large, soft towel behind her shoulders and then used each end to pull her to him. 'I'm not really such an ogre, you know.'

When their bodies met she closed her eyes. Perhaps if she couldn't see him she wouldn't respond. What a futile thought. Sensation sizzled through every vein, heating her skin with incredible speed. His body was hard against her much softer one, and she wanted to maintain that contact. It filled her with desire so deep that it threatened to destroy her.

This was insanity; she had to free herself. 'Thank you,' she said, alarmed to hear how husky her voice sounded. 'I can manage.'

Amazingly he let her go without a struggle, still with that knowing smile. Nothing she did escaped him. He knew her so well that he could probably read her mind even when she was absent.

'It's late,' she whispered. 'I'm going to bed. Thank you again for cleaning the pool.'

'The pleasure's mine.'

But whether he meant cleaning the pool or swimming with her, or even looking at her as he was doing now with that smile in his eyes, she had no way of knowing. She turned her back and hurried indoors, wishing, not for the first time, that there was a lock on her bedroom door.

She took the quickest shower ever, half expecting him to join her, thankful when he didn't. In fact, when she looked out of her bedroom window he was still standing at the water's edge, a pool of water at his feet reflecting the brilliance of the moon. He'd been swimming again! To cool his ardour? Or weren't his feelings the same as hers? Was he simply playing with her?

Not expecting to sleep, Leanne knew nothing more until Courtney bounced into her room at half-past seven the following morning. 'Leanne, Leanne, I want to swim.'

Leanne forced open tired eyelids. 'Ask Josh.' She didn't want to get up yet—she'd been in the middle of a beautiful dream in which she and Joshua were still married, still living in London, and she'd just announced that she was pregnant. She'd been awaiting his reaction.

'Josh isn't here.'

Forced to wake up properly, Leanne frowned. 'Where is he?'

'Gone. Don't know.'

Leanne scrambled out of bed and peered through her window. But the pool was still; not a ripple disturbed its surface. He'd probably gone to the plant to check that the men were all there on time and working properly. It had become a habit with him to wander down there early.

'OK,' she said, 'run and find your swimmers. But after breakfast I'm going to be busy. Molly's coming to look after you.'

'Goodie.' Courtney clapped her hands together. 'I like Molly. Molly's funny. Can she swim with me?'

'You'll have to ask her that.'

Joshua turned up for breakfast, apologised to Courtney for letting her down, and then disappeared again. Leanne wondered why he was in such a rush. Not that she dwelt on it; she'd got used to Joshua putting his heart and soul into his work.

She spent her entire morning sorting out her mother's sewing room. Molly made lunch but Leanne ate alone. Courtney had tired herself out and was fast asleep, and Molly was now baking a batch of cakes. She was so good, thought Leanne as she nibbled a crispbread and picked at the cheese and salad. A real stalwart in times of need.

Mid-afternoon the computer arrived, followed shortly afterwards by the desk, and by the time Joshua arrived home she had everything set up.

'You did this?' he asked. 'Why? I would have done it for you.'

'As you didn't turn up for lunch, I suspected you were deeply involved in something. I didn't want to trouble you. In any case I'm perfectly capable.'

'So I see,' he said with admiration in his eyes. 'And everything I ordered for the office has arrived as well. How long will it take for you to work out a programme?'

'Weeks probably,' she said with a laugh. 'I can't conjure it up out of thin air. I'll need to go through things with you some more before I even start.'

'We could go back there now.'

'No!' she declared emphatically. 'There's no urgency as far as I can see.'

'I think there is,' he muttered, but that was all he said.

Leanne worked hard in the days that followed. She settled into a routine of swimming with Courtney every morning before breakfast, and every evening with Joshua. They laughed a lot and talked a lot but he never made a pass at her. Not that he wouldn't have liked to, she knew that; she could see it in his eyes, in the way he sometimes made a movement towards her and then changed his mind. For some reason he was respecting her wishes and for that she was thankful.

And slowly she was getting over the trauma of her mother's death. Having work to do helped, and Molly was a godsend. She kept Courtney away from her while she was working, but she never let the child feel pushed out.

Sometimes they would peep round the door of the sewing room and Courtney would blow her a kiss and say, 'I love you,' and then run away again. And sometimes Leanne would see her on her swing or her slide with Molly supervising. Life was beginning to feel good.

Ivan came to see her practically every day and always asked her out, but invariably she refused. She didn't want to build up his hopes when there were none. He'd sit and have a beer and would often be deep in thought.

'How's Joshua doing?' she asked one day, wondering if he was the person worrying Ivan.

'He's like a rat up a drainpipe; he leaves nothing unturned.'

It was said so fiercely that Leanne looked at him in concern. 'Is he upsetting the workers?'

'He's upsetting me,' muttered Ivan. 'He's quietly taking over my job.'

'I'm sure that's not his intention,' said Leanne at once. 'He just wants to learn everything as quickly as possible.'

'He's taken you off me as well.'

This did have Leanne sitting to attention. 'What do you mean?'

'It's obvious. You won't go out with me any more. I'd begun to think that we were getting close. I thought you liked me. In fact I thought you were beginning to fall in love with me. Leanne, I was going to ask you to marry me. Do I stand a chance?'

CHAPTER EIGHT

LEANNE would have loved to be able to say yes, if only to keep Joshua off her back. But that wouldn't be fair and so she slowly shook her head. 'I love you as a friend, Ivan, and I hope you'll always remain that, but as for anything else, I'm sorry.'

'It's still Joshua, isn't it?'

'No!' She shook her head emphatically. 'I don't love him either.'

'So maybe there is hope?' There was such an earnest expression on his face that Leanne felt guilty.

'Maybe,' she admitted. 'But don't get too excited.'

'I won't.' But he looked happier than when he had arrived.

Leanne's main problem was Joshua and her crazy need of him. The fact that he was down at the winery almost all of each day helped, but sometimes she sat at the computer and instead of working found herself daydreaming about making love with him.

The signals her body sent out were so intense that they alarmed her. And yet they were also so very natural that she began to wonder why she shouldn't have a physical relationship with him. Nothing else, no commitment—he wouldn't want that anyway. They were two people trapped, if that was the right word, in a space capsule of time. Both with needs that wanted fulfilling.

It wouldn't be forever, she was sure of that. Joshua

would get fed up of playing the wine game; he would want to return to his homeland, check that Mark was running the company properly, settle back into London life. She found it hard to believe that he wasn't missing it.

She put the question to him one evening after they'd had their, by now, customary swim and were relaxing on canvas chairs at the poolside with their towels draped around their shoulders. A flock of sulphur-crested cockatoos were squabbling noisily in the treetops, as they did every evening at dusk.

'Yes, I suppose I do it miss it,' he answered. 'But not in the sense that I want to go back. Maybe I'm getting too old for that frenetic lifestyle; I don't know. What I do know is that I love it out here.'

Leanne felt faint unease. 'Are you saying that you'd like to make Australia your permanent home?'

He looked at her with his head to one side, a considering gleam in his eyes. 'You don't fancy the idea?'

'It's your choice,' she said with a faint shrug. There was nothing she could do to stop him. 'I suppose if you did you'd sell your apartment and buy a place of your own.'

'You're kicking me out?'

'I didn't say that,' she retorted quickly. 'But if you're going to put down roots...' She let her sentence fade away. She didn't want Joshua as a permanent lodger, not even as a live-in lover—exciting though the thought was. Hatred and resentment still simmered. She would never get over the hurt he had inflicted. Never! Not if she lived to be a hundred.

He sat forward on the edge of his seat and, taking

her hands into his, he looked deep into her eyes. 'I know how you feel. I know how much I've hurt you.'

Oh, lord, the sob story. He wanted to kiss and make up. As if! Not in a million years. 'You've no idea how I feel,' she snapped. 'You hurt me beyond measure.' She tried to pull free but he would have none of it. His grip tightened and he compelled her to look at him.

Leanne saw passion in his eyes. Not desire, not lust, but a different kind of passion. An intensity that was disturbing.

'Maybe this isn't the time or place, in fact I know it's not, but it needs to be said. There'll never be a right time so I may as well do it now.'

There was a stillness about him and Leanne sensed that whatever it was he wanted to say she wouldn't like it. He was going to hurt her some more! This time she did manage to snatch free. 'I don't want to hear it,' she spat, clapping her hands over her ears. 'Whatever it is, keep it to yourself. And maybe this *would* be a good time for you to move out. It isn't working, us living together.'

He frowned. 'Who says?'

'*I* do! I'm on edge all the time. Living with an ex-husband is hardly the ideal situation. I must have been crazy to agree to it.'

'Not crazy,' he said softly. 'I'm the one who's crazy for throwing you out in the first place.'

Leanne's brows lifted and she looked at him cautiously. 'What's this? An apology? If it is you can stuff it. I don't want it; it's far too late for anything like that.'

'Hear me out, please.'

'Why should I?' She suddenly shivered and Joshua sprang up.

'You're cold. Let's go indoors and get you out of that wet swimsuit.'

'Out of my swimsuit, yes, but into my bed—that's where I'm going,' she riposted. 'Alone!' She added this last for good measure in case he got any wrong ideas.

'You're not going to bed until you hear what I've got to say,' he told her tersely.

They both went to their rooms to shower and change and Joshua determined that if Leanne didn't join him afterwards then he would jolly well go and fetch her. It was time for him to tell her about Mark's confession.

He'd come to the conclusion that she and Ivan weren't as close as she would have him believe. There had been no further evenings out, and although Ivan had gone to the house with alarming regularity, and he'd been tempted to follow to see exactly what was going on, it had always been when Molly and Courtney were home as well, so there would have been no chance for them to make love.

Not that Ivan wouldn't have liked it to happen, of that Joshua was sure. Leanne would be a good catch if he could win her. But Joshua also felt certain that Leanne wasn't truly interested. Maybe that one time they'd gone to bed together she'd realised Ivan couldn't raise her to the heights that he did. The thought brought a pleased smile to his lips. It was why he had decided that now was the time to talk.

He returned to the lounge room, poured himself a

glass of Scotch and sank into one of the easy chairs. As he waited Joshua rested his head back and closed his eyes, and was almost asleep when he became aware of Leanne standing beside him.

Watching her through half-closed lids, he saw her turn away. He stretched out his arm and caught her wrist. 'Oh, no, you don't.'

'I thought you were asleep,' she said quietly.

'I was beginning to think that I'd have to come and fetch you.' She looked stunning in a silver-grey caftan. Her feet were bare, her face scrubbed clean, her wild blonde hair, still wet from the shower, combed severely back and fixed in a band of some description. He had never seen her look more beautiful.

Her eyes were troubled, though, and he wanted to take that away from her. He wanted her to be happy; gloriously happy, the way she had been in the first days of their marriage. 'What would you like to drink?' he asked.

'Nothing, thank you,' and she moved across the room to drop into the chair furthest away from him.

Not a good sign. 'Some ginger wine perhaps?' He knew she liked that.

'No,' she returned crisply. 'Just say what you've got to say and let me go to bed.'

She was making this hard for him. He would have liked her at his side, he would have liked to hold her hand while he was talking. He didn't want to shout Mark's confession across the room. So he stood up and walked slowly over to her, but he didn't sit down, he stood there looking down at her and he could smell the clean freshness of her and his whole body shivered inside. He wanted her so much.

'How close are you and Ivan?' were his first words. 'And I want the truth.'

Leanne looked wary, he thought, her eyes widening as she looked up at him. 'Close enough; why?'

'It's important to me.'

'Important?' she flared. 'When has anything I did been important to you? You relinquished the right to care about what I do or what I feel years ago.'

Yes, he had, and now he felt truly dreadful about it. 'Maybe I want to take up that right again,' he said softly.

'And pigs might fly,' she jeered. 'If that's what this is all about then forget it.' She put her hands on the arm of the chair and began to push herself up.

Joshua touched her shoulder. 'It's not. Stay there and listen.'

With clear reluctance she sank back into her seat, but she sat stiff and unyielding. This was going to be harder than he'd expected. Her lovely eyes were shooting sparks of anger and he knew that he would have to choose his words carefully if he didn't want to destroy their relationship altogether.

'I had a long talk with Mark while I was in England.'

'Good for you,' she snapped. 'Did he tell more lies about me?'

'On the contrary.' He dragged up a stool and squatted on the edge of it in front of her. 'He confessed the truth.'

Leanne's eyes snapped even wider. 'That was big of him.'

'I should have listened to you, I should have known that—'

'But you didn't, did you?' she protested fiercely. 'You put me through hell instead. I couldn't care less what Mark's said to you; the cold, hard fact is that you wouldn't take my word, you didn't trust me. That hurt, Josh; you'll never know how much.'

At the time he'd been hurting too. His whole world had come crashing down and he hadn't really thought about her feelings. He was the one who had been betrayed, it was his life that was falling apart—and he had blamed her for it. All the more so because he had never expected anything like that of her. In his eyes she had been perfection personified. And when that conviction was smashed into pieces his mind was in such torment that clear thinking was out of the question.

'I want to make it up to you,' he said gruffly.

'I bet you do,' she snapped. 'I don't know why you've even told me because it makes no difference. It's over, Joshua. Everything we had going for us is gone, forever. And you did it with your narrow-mindedness, so don't try and think a few fancy words will make any difference now.'

Joshua felt stone-cold inside. Never had he heard her more determined. The only good thing in all of this was that she was still physically attracted to him, and if he had to use this as a way of persuasion, then he would. But at this stage he didn't want to go down that road. He wanted her to accept that he was truly sorry, he wanted her to understand that it had cost him dear too and he was prepared to go to whatever lengths were needed to build back the deeply loving relationship they'd once had.

'Leanne.' He would have taken her hands if she

hadn't tucked them away. 'Leanne, please, listen to me. I love you from the bottom of my heart. I thought that love had gone away, I admit that, but it hasn't. It's still there, and if I have to grovel on my knees for the rest of my life then I'll do it if it will make you believe that I am truly, truly sorry. I must have been an idiot to believe Mark over you—'

'You were,' she cut in viciously. 'The world's worst. And I will never, ever forgive you. So you may as well stop wasting your breath.'

Her cruel words slashed into him like a knife blade. He could feel his blood running icy cold. 'I understand how you must feel,' he said gruffly through a throat that was tight with fear. 'And I'm in the depths of anguish myself. I'm guilty, I admit that. I should be hung, drawn and quartered for what I did to you, and I know you'll never forgive me, but surely you can find it in your heart to at least begin to relent. I can't go on living without you.'

'Tell me,' she said, her eyes full of scorn, 'would you have ever come to find me if our parents hadn't died? Would we have been having this conversation?' She didn't wait for him to answer. 'I don't think so. I think that maybe you still find me physically attractive, as I do you, but that's no basis for a lasting relationship.'

Joshua closed his eyes for a second or two, drawing in a deep, unsteady breath. 'At least say you'll think about it,' he said hoarsely. He hadn't expected her to be quite so adamant. In all honesty, though, he couldn't blame her. He would feel the same if their positions were reversed. 'You're not making this easy for me, Leanne.'

'I have no intention of making it easy,' she claimed, 'and I really don't see what there is to think about. I've given you my answer.'

'You didn't respond when I asked you how involved you were with Ivan.'

She gave a tiny huff down her nose. 'If I say that I'm deeply involved, will you go away?'

'No, because I know he's not right for you.'

'Then answering your question is pointless.'

'At least I'd know what I'm up against.'

'You're up against me,' she spat furiously. 'Me alone. Me and my anger. Me and my hatred. And who's to say that Mark isn't lying again? Maybe he's doing it because he's now happily married and wants to see you happy. Maybe he thinks it will help. Maybe we did have an affair. How will you ever know the real truth? I know for a fact that you'll never believe anything I tell you.'

Joshua abruptly stood up and took a few steps across the room before turning to face her, every ounce of colour drained from his face. He clenched his jaw, feeling muscles jerking; even his heart was slamming around behind his breastbone. This was a slant he hadn't thought of. 'I don't give a damn whether you had an affair or not. Not any longer. It's irrelevant. It's what I feel in here—' he banged his fist against his chest '—that's important.'

'Really?' She allowed her finely plucked brows to rise in disbelief. 'You could have fooled me. What you felt in there was distrust, and if you've felt it once you can feel it again. You'll never trust me. I'd only have to look at another man and you'd think I was bedding him. Do you think I want to lead that sort of life?'

Joshua wasn't prepared to give up but he could see that there was no point in him pressing the matter any further at this moment. And he wasn't even sure whether talking would do the trick. He had never known her so adamant. And, dammit, it was his fault. He was the one who had done the damage, he had been unforgivably cruel; how he was ever going to redeem himself he had no idea. It looked as though using their highly charged physical needs as persuasion might be his only option.

'Why didn't you tell me about your conversation with Mark when you first came back?' Leanne had stood up too and was now looking at him icily, her hands on her hips, her feet apart.

Oh, how he longed to take her into his arms, to smooth away that troubled crease on her forehead, banish every bad thought she harboured. It was like wishing for the moon. 'I fully intended to, but I found you in Ivan's arms and decided to wait until a more appropriate time.'

'Appropriate,' she jeered, 'would mean never. And I wish you hadn't told me because it makes absolutely no difference to the way I feel. Goodnight, Josh; I'm going to bed.'

She swept past him with such hauteur that he couldn't help but admire her, and it took every ounce of his self-control not to follow. But he'd said enough for now; there was always another day.

Leanne couldn't sleep. She'd been surprised to hear that Mark had finally confessed, although she shouldn't have been because he'd already said he wanted to. But seeing Joshua Powers actually apologising had somehow tugged at her heartstrings.

He was normally such an arrogant, self-confident man, never giving an inch in any direction. How much had it cost him to plead with her? Not that she was in any danger of giving way. She was absolutely positive that he would always be wary, always on the lookout for any signs that she was seeing another man.

Take Ivan for instance; look how Joshua had added up what he had seen and come up with the wrong answer. And he would come up with the wrong answer every time. Her life wouldn't be worth living. She had most definitely done the right thing in rejecting him.

How she was going to get over the sexual hurdle was another matter. She wasn't naïve enough to believe that he wouldn't try it on again. And she certainly wouldn't be strong enough to refuse him. But maybe, a very big maybe, if she gave it long enough they would burn themselves out.

When one o'clock passed and then two, and the bed was nothing more than a heap of crumpled sheets and a pillow that had been pummelled to death, Leanne decided to get up and make herself a drink of hot milk. She tiptoed into the kitchen without putting on any lights, shrieking in alarm when she bumped into a warm, firm body.

'Hey there,' Joshua said gruffly, 'what are you doing, creeping around at this time of night?'

As he held her steady Leanne's whole body leapt into response mode. She was wearing next to nothing and neither, it appeared, was Joshua. At least, he wore nothing on his top half; she didn't dare look down any further.

'I wanted a glass of milk.' Something she could make more quickly. Anything to get away from him before the unimaginable happened.

'Then let me do the honours.'

He opened the fridge and as the light angled into the room she saw that he was, as she had feared, stark naked. With a little squeak she turned and ran.

CHAPTER NINE

'LEANNE!'

Joshua's voice arrested her. Leanne halted but didn't turn around. She didn't want to look at him because she knew what his naked body would do to her, what it was already doing! It was creating a maelstrom of feelings over which she had absolutely no control.

'Leanne, don't go.' He strode across the room and she turned quickly because otherwise she knew that she would end up imprisoned against that sexy, dangerously hard body. He was not in the least inhibited by his nakedness. The fridge door was still open, back-lighting him. She could see the beautiful, strong shape of him, she could see his tousled hair that looked as though he had run his fingers through it a million times. She curled her fingers into her palms, knowing already what the outcome was going to be.

'Tell me why you couldn't sleep.'

He was close to her now, so close that she could hear him breathing. And she could smell the seductive maleness of him. It had been a mistake waiting, not rushing away to her room where she could shut him out. Not that a closed door would have been much help. The feelings were there, they refused to go away, and whether he was standing next to her or a hundred metres distant it would make no difference.

'I think you know the answer to that,' she answered

crisply. 'It wasn't the sort of conversation I like late at night.'

'Did it make any difference,' he asked softly, 'lying there in your bed thinking about it? Have you changed your mind?'

She shook her head firmly. 'No! Never! All the apologies in the world will make no difference.'

'Perhaps this will.' His voice was nothing more than a sexy growl as he slid one arm behind her back and the other hand behind her head. She was urged against his powerful body, his mouth laid claim to hers, and the next second she was his. She hadn't the power to resist. He had already woven his spell over her by simply being there.

Delicious shudder followed delicious shudder. This wouldn't end here, she knew that. And for the moment she didn't care. She accepted his thrusting tongue; she lifted a leg and rubbed it against his; she luxuriated in the hard, masculine power of him.

Her whole body throbbed as his hands caressed, as there was no inch left untouched. Sex with Joshua had always been her downfall. It was impossible to deny him no matter what. And he knew it. And he was taking advantage. And there was nothing she could do to stop him.

When he lifted her into his arms and carried her through to his bedroom she felt as though she was living a dream. None of it was real. It couldn't be. She didn't want this to happen. She would wake up soon in her own bed.

But meantime she was eager to accept all that Joshua offered. He stripped off her nightie and laid her down gently, and then he stood looking down.

His eyes sought out every intimate spot and aroused her perhaps even more than if he'd touched her. She began to writhe on the bed and held out her arms for him to come to her.

It was with excruciating slowness that he did so. He seemed to hesitate for so long that she began to wonder whether this was what he really wanted. Then the familiar slow, deadly smile spread across his face, his eyes seduced her, and urgent desire took over.

She would never, in a thousand years, get tired of his lovemaking, thought Leanne, so there flew out of the window the thought that they'd burn themselves out. There was no backing down now, though. She needed this man to assuage the fierce need that burnt inside her.

Their lovemaking had never been more intense or more satisfying than it was that night. They made love almost continuously. Sometimes hot and steamy, at others simply touching and stroking. Touching with their fingers, touching with their tongues, reacquainting themselves with every inch of each other's bodies. It was excruciatingly beautiful.

They didn't speak much. Leanne was afraid to. She didn't want to spoil anything. Tomorrow she would regret it, she knew that, but tonight was one of those occasions she wanted to slip into her book of memories. Only very special events went in there. Like camping in the outback on her twelfth birthday. A surprise sixteenth-birthday party. The day she met Josh. The day they married. When he had taken her on a cruise down the Thames. Perfect memories.

She couldn't remember when they both drifted to

sleep. The first thing she knew was when Courtney touched her shoulder and called her name.

'Sweetheart, what is it?' she asked at once.

'I couldn't find you.'

And then she remembered where she was and swift colour flamed her cheeks. Feeling cautiously with her leg, she discovered to her relief that Joshua had gone.

'Why are you sleeping in Josh's bed?'

''Cos I couldn't sleep, little one. Do you remember when you couldn't sleep and I climbed into your bed? It's the same thing.'

Courtney nodded, happily accepting the explanation. 'Molly's here. She says—shall she cook breakfast?'

Normally Leanne had eaten by the time Molly arrived and she felt embarrassed to be found still in bed. So long as Molly didn't know in whose bed she was!

'I'm not hungry, sweetheart. Tell her I'll get myself something later.'

Courtney ran happily away and Leanne fled to her own room. What a night! She could quite easily have curled up and gone to sleep again, she was so tired. Her body felt good, though. It felt—and she hated to use the word—but it felt loved.

Joshua had actually said that he still loved her, but it wasn't love they'd experienced in his bed, it was pure, unadulterated sex. Something she could become addicted to if she wasn't careful. And without a doubt it would create the wrong impression. Joshua would think that she was weakening, that there could be a chance of her learning to love him again.

Love! She tossed the word round and round in her mind. He didn't know the meaning of the word. Love meant loving someone despite their faults. Love meant trusting them through thick and thin.

For five long years he hadn't given her a second thought. How could that be love? Joshua used the word too easily. He wanted her body, the same as she wanted his. That was all there was to it. And with that she could live.

By the time Joshua came up to the house for his lunch Leanne had herself under control again. Molly had surpassed herself with a salmon mousse and green salad, followed by mango cheesecake, and Leanne ate hungrily.

Joshua watched her and smiled. 'You know what they say about women who shovel food down their throats as though there's no tomorrow—I'm beginning to believe it's true.'

Leanne frowned. 'What do they say?' and then as the innuendo hit her she flashed her green eyes. 'This is simply because I missed breakfast.'

'Why was that, I wonder, my delightful lover? You looked so beautiful and innocent in your sleep that I almost woke you so that we could start over again.'

Leanne's hormones jumped, startled into rapid arousal.

'But then I thought that perhaps I'd better let you replenish yourself, ready for tonight.'

'Tonight?' she echoed. 'I'm not sleeping with you again.'

'No?' He lifted a sardonic brow.

'No!' she confirmed, horrified at the way her body was behaving.

'I think maybe you won't be able to help yourself,' he murmured, stroking her arm with the tips of his fingers. 'You're one hell of a sexy lady, Leanne. You always were, but if anything our parting has made you even hungrier. You were magnificent last night.'

And so was he. Insatiable. Unsurpassable. So why deny herself? Because she was afraid, that was why. Because she might relent, because she might mistake sex for love. She gave a tiny shake of her head. 'It was a one-off.' And would he please stop touching her, stop stimulating her senses?

His smile was slow and confident, and also very, very sexy. 'If that was a one-off then it should be repeated. It was spectacularly wonderful. Don't you agree?'

How could she not? 'It always has been.'

'And could you bear to give that up?'

'It's not really a choice I have. I want a proper relationship with someone. I don't want one that's going nowhere.'

'It doesn't have to be that way,' he answered quietly, a faint pained expression in his eyes. 'We could still have a good life together. I know that it was through my own stupidity that I ruined it, but in time I'm sure—'

'In time, nothing,' she flashed back. 'You know my feelings on that score. Nothing will change them.'

And in the days that followed she kept to her promise. She still swam with Joshua, still sat and talked, but always she ran away to her room before he could begin to work his magic on her.

Joshua was deeply disappointed that he was getting nowhere with Leanne. He hadn't expected it to be easy, but neither had he thought she would distance herself from him. Especially after the night they'd spent together. He really had thought that it was the beginning of something good.

Clearly she was scared by how much of herself she'd revealed and had correspondingly withdrawn into her shell. It was going to take a great deal of patience on his part to win her over. And did he have that patience? It definitely wasn't one of his strongest virtues.

He threw himself even more deeply into his work. He found the whole wine industry totally fascinating and didn't mind how many hours he worked. He couldn't wait for Leanne to finish the programme. He felt constricted with the present system. In his eyes it was totally out of date. Why scribble in ledgers and books when it could all be keyed into the system and processed for you? It would make life easier all round. Surely Ivan could see that?

Unless of course there was a very good reason why Ivan didn't want to change. Joshua had insisted on a stock take and it didn't add up. And when he had asked questions Ivan was the only man who had looked faintly guilty. Of course, without proof he couldn't say anything, and it was doubtful Leanne would believe him if he did. She would think it was sour grapes. She would think he was doing it to discredit Ivan, hoping to get rid of him so that he, Joshua, would stand a better chance.

Over dinner one evening Leanne shocked him by saying that she was going away for the weekend. His immediate thought was that she was going somewhere with Ivan and he felt a stone-cold dread inside his stomach. But he let none of his dismay show.

'That's nice,' he said instead. 'You deserve some relaxation. Where are you going?'

'Sydney.'

'Sydney?' he echoed. 'That's a long way, surely, for a weekend?'

'I'm flying.'

I, not we, he noticed. Did that mean he was worrying for nothing?

'I'm going to visit an old school-friend who I haven't seen for almost two years.'

His relief was almost palpable. 'Have you booked your flight yet?'

Leanne shook her head.

'Then let's make it a flight for two. My shout. It's about time I saw some more of your beautiful country.'

'Joshua! I can't do that,' declared Leanne, a look of horror on her face. 'I can't ask Cindy to put you up as well. In any case we have loads to catch up on. You'd find it extremely boring.'

'I don't find anything I do with you boring,' he announced with a smile. 'You should know that.'

'I know that you're a persistent devil,' she protested. 'Hasn't it occurred to you that's it you I want to get away from for a couple of days?'

Oh, yes, it had occurred to him all right. He knew exactly what thoughts were going through Leanne's head. But if she thought she would get rid of him that way then she was deeply mistaken. 'I promise I won't get in your way. I'll book into a hotel. I won't even see you for the entire weekend if that's your wish. I'll explore Sydney on my own. Of course, it won't be so much fun, but—'

'Stop that!' she declared angrily, her lovely eyes flashing her disapproval.

'So do we have a date?' He held his breath as he waited for her answer.

'It doesn't look as though I'm going to be able to stop you,' she hissed.

Lord, she looked beautiful. When she was angry her whole body became vibrantly alive. There was an electric quality about her. She lit up like a neon sign. It had been several days now since she had let him near her and he felt his testosterone levels rising sky-high. Perhaps when they went for their swim later...

But his hopes were dashed when she ran swiftly into the house immediately they climbed out of the pool. She was making it very clear that she wasn't happy with the thought of him accompanying her to Sydney. Not that it mattered; he intended going with her whatever she said.

He sat out on the veranda, deliberately choosing a spot close to Leanne's window, and listened to see whether she was slamming around in her room or whether all was silent and she was already asleep.

It was silent.

But he couldn't rest. He didn't like the way she had run out on him, as if she was afraid. Afraid of what, for pity's sake? He wasn't going to harm her; all he wanted was a good relationship, something he could build on, but she was acting as though he intended her harm.

He had never wished that on her, not even when he'd kicked her out of his house. Joshua winced as he thought of that terrible day when Mark had told him he'd made love to his wife, and he'd gone racing home to confront her.

She'd denied it so vehemently and yet still he had disbelieved her. His own wife, the woman he loved more than anything else in the world—and he hadn't believed her. What an idiot. What a complete and utter fool. And now it was beginning to look as though he would never win her back.

Maybe the trip to Sydney would do the trick. Somewhere far away so that she couldn't hide behind Ivan. The tickets were booked. They flew first thing on Saturday morning. But there were still a couple of days to get through and he wanted to sort things out with Leanne before they went. He didn't want to spend the whole weekend winning her round. He wanted it to be perfect in every way.

He wasn't sure what this Cindy woman was like. Leanne had mentioned her a couple of times in the past. She was her best friend from school, had married a banker from Sydney, and they rarely saw each other now. He hoped she would be accommodating enough to let him spend some time with Leanne on his own.

Finally he strode into the house and tapped on Leanne's door. When she didn't answer he opened it and peered inside. But instead of finding her asleep he saw she was curled up on a chair with a magazine. She wasn't reading it; it was flat on her lap, and there was aggression in her eyes as he stepped into the room and closed the door behind him.

'What are you doing here?' she asked curtly.

'What are you doing hiding yourself away from me?' he countered. 'Are you scared?'

'Of course not,' she scorned. 'What I don't like is

the way you try to force yourself on me every time we're alone.'

Joshua let out a swift hiss through his teeth. She certainly knew how to hit below the belt. 'Force?' he enquired harshly. 'I don't ever remember using force where you're concerned. And if I wanted to take you now I wouldn't have to use force. Admit it. You're as hungry for me as I am for you. If there's nothing else going in our favour it's that.'

'Maybe,' she huffed, 'but it doesn't mean I support it. In fact the more I think about it the more repulsed I am. I find it hard to believe that my body acts in defiance to my mind.'

Joshua didn't believe that it did. She was compelling herself to accept that she no longer felt anything for him. It was a feel-safe theory. But in truth both her body and mind still belonged to him. Their separation had done nothing to diminish Leanne's feelings, or his own. He loved her as much as ever, possibly more so, and he was willing to bet every last penny he possessed that she still loved him.

If only there was some way he could convince her of it, some way to make it up to her.

'So what you're saying is that you're going to shut yourself away from me at every opportunity just in case your body lets you down?' he enquired tersely. 'Don't you think that's taking things too far?'

Leanne lifted her shoulders and let them drop slowly. 'It's for the best.'

'For whom?'

'Me, of course. You know perfectly well that you have the power to make me do things I don't want to do.'

Power! Over Leanne! Hmm. If he did have it, which he doubted very much, it didn't do him any good. If he had the power she spoke of then she'd be his again now. Leanne was the one with the power. Power over mind. She was determined not to give in to him, and in any other circumstances that determination would have done her credit. Today it merely frustrated him.

'Are you happy, Leanne?'

His question took her by surprise and she shot him a startled glance. 'Reasonably so, I suppose,' she answered reluctantly.

'But not as happy as when we were first married, when we met, in fact?'

'Absolutely not,' she retorted, 'and you know why. Can't you get it into your thick skull that you hurt me? So much so that I can never forgive you.'

'Never is a long time.' His gut ached at the thought that she would never, ever learn to love him again. It twisted into knots. They had reached an impasse. And it would take every ounce of his ingenuity and cunning and tact and patience to win her over again. Did he have those qualities?

He wanted to go to her now. He wanted to take her hands and lift her up from the chair and hold her against him. He wanted to feel the rapid beat of her heart, the warmth of her skin, the way her body trembled when she was aroused. He wanted to swear to her that he would never hurt her again. And most of all he wanted to make love to her.

'You should have thought of that before you exiled me,' she told him testily.

'I made a mistake.' A monumental one, one that

he would remember with regret for the rest of his life. 'I'm only human, Leanne.' But he wasn't prepared to give up, oh, no. Those few days in Sydney were going to be make or break time; he was determined on that score.

'Cindy, this is Joshua.'

Joshua saw the surprise on Cindy's face, the unspoken words. Joshua? *The* Joshua? Your ex-husband? What's going on?

The look in her blue eyes made him smile.

'Yes, I'm the one,' he said.

'But I didn't know that—'

'We're not,' Leanne told her abruptly. 'Josh is helping run the winery but that's all.'

So why is he here? asked the blue eyes.

'He wants to see Sydney,' Leanne informed in response to the unspoken question.

'Then I'm the right girl to show you!' exclaimed Cindy at once. 'I hope you haven't booked into a hotel because you can stay with us; we have plenty of room.'

Joshua saw Leanne's dismay but this was exactly what he had hoped for. He smiled broadly. 'That's very kind of you, Cindy. To tell you the truth I wasn't looking forward to wandering around on my own.'

'You don't mind, Leanne?' asked Cindy as an apparent afterthought.

Leanne gave an indifferent shrug. 'Not if you don't. But what will Bob say?'

'He'll enjoy having another man in the house. Bob's very much into golf, Joshua. Do you play?'

'I've been known to have the odd game but it's not

a passion of mine.' Leanne was his passion. He had no real interest in anything other than persuading her to share his life again. He wanted marriage. He wanted children. He wanted her to forgive him.

They made their way to Cindy's car and she drove with amazing speed and dexterity to a house overlooking Sydney Harbour. 'Here we are. Can you manage the cases, Joshua?'

'This is some place you have here,' he said as he nodded and lifted them out. 'Stunning views. My own place has views but they're over the London skyline, not your beautiful harbour.'

'The best in the world,' she boasted and then laughed. 'I bet you've heard that a few times?'

'Indeed. Do you have your own boat?'

'Naturally, though Bob never lets me take it out alone. I can't think why.'

If she drove it as hard as she did her car then Joshua could understand her husband's reservations. 'Are you sure he won't mind me staying here?'

'Not at all. Now, are you two sharing a room or—?'

'No, we're not,' said Leanne in such a sharp tone that Cindy raised a brow.

'Then you take this room, Joshua, and Leanne, yours is next door. They both overlook the water so there'll be no reason to argue.'

Joshua smiled appreciatively but Leanne scowled and swiftly disappeared. She was making it perfectly clear that it hadn't been her idea for him to tag along. He hoped she wasn't going to be like this the whole weekend.

*   *   *

'What a cutie,' said Cindy. 'How could you bear to leave him? And why are you giving him the cold shoulder now?'

Leanne had gone downstairs and joined her friend outside by the pool. A huge canvas sail shielded them from the baking sun and a jug of ice-cold lemonade sat on a table at their sides, together with a dish of freshly sliced fruit.

'You know what he did to me.'

'Well, yes, but it looks to me as though he wants to make amends.'

'He does.'

'So what's the problem? He's gorgeous. I tell you what, you take Bob and I'll have Joshua.'

Leanne laughed because Bob was anything but handsome. He made up for it in other ways, though. He was a thoughtful, caring husband who doted on his wife and would do anything for her. He was well-respected at work as well, and sat on many committees. Some people saw him as dull but he wasn't. He had a dry sense of humour and he and Cindy had lots of friends.

'You're welcome to Joshua,' she said now. 'I shall never trust him again.'

'Never is a long time, Leanne. Most of us make mistakes. The question is, do we learn by them? Don't you think Joshua has learnt?'

'I don't know,' she answered slowly, 'but if I give him a second chance and he hasn't then I'll be hurt all over again. I don't want that to happen.'

'But you still love him?'

Leanne shook her head. 'My feelings for him have gone forever.'

'All of them?' asked Cindy archly.

Leanne was saved answering when Joshua appeared silently at their sides. They both had their backs to the house and hadn't realised he was approaching. Had he heard any of their conversation? Not that it mattered; he knew exactly how she felt and if he had listened then it would only have confirmed what she'd already told him.

'May I?' He picked up a glass and the jug of lemonade.

'Help yourself,' said Cindy pleasantly. 'We were just talking about you. I was going to swap you for Bob.'

His rugged brows rose and his eyes twinkled. 'Now, there's an interesting idea. What would Bob say, do you think?'

'I think,' she said slowly, 'that he'd get out his shotgun.'

Joshua's laughter filled the air and Leanne felt a ripple of pain inside her. It had been so long since she'd heard him laugh like that—except when he was playing with Courtney. At one time laughter had played a large part in their lives. Now neither of them seemed to laugh any more.

And why did she care? He could laugh or cry or do whatever he liked; it didn't matter to her. Did it?

'Where's Bob by the way?' Joshua asked.

'Can't you guess?' asked Cindy. 'Playing golf. It was fixed before Leanne said she was coming. And because he knows how much we like girlie talk he didn't feel it necessary to change his plans.'

'And I spoilt them for you. Should I take a walk, do you think? Let you carry on talking about me?'

'We're saying nothing that you don't already know,' answered Leanne sharply.

'Have some fruit,' said Cindy quickly, offering Joshua the dish. 'I hadn't realised you were in the wine trade too.'

'I'm not, but I'm learning.'

'And are you enjoying it?'

'Tremendously.'

'And do you plan to remain in Australia, or will your business interests in London call you back?'

In other words, thought Leanne, what were his intentions where she was concerned? Cindy was anything but subtle. And she had an insatiable curiosity.

'I've not yet made up my mind,' answered Joshua with a slow smile and a sideways glance at Leanne.

Meaning that it was all down to her! 'My mother and Joshua's father left us half shares,' she explained. 'So we either go along with it or one buys the other out. And as I haven't the money…'

'And as Joshua clearly doesn't wish to leave you to run it alone…' expanded Cindy.

'We have a lot to sort out.'

'Sounds like fun,' declared the brunette flippantly. 'But you, Joshua, don't strike me as the sort of man who'd be satisfied with half of a small company. Not even the whole of it. I imagine you'd have your sights set much higher. Am I right?'

'You're a shrewd judge of character,' he said with a smile and a nod, 'considering you've only just met me.'

'So what are your long-term plans?'

Joshua looked at Leanne and she quailed under the intensity of his gaze. Even before he spoke she knew what he was going to say and it sent a river of nervousness through her limbs. For an instant she wished that she had something stronger to drink than lemonade.

'To remarry Leanne.'

CHAPTER TEN

THERE was a moment's silence between the three of them. Cindy was stunned, Joshua was expectant and Leanne felt embarrassed that he had been so outspoken to someone he had been introduced to only a few hours ago.

'Well,' said Cindy, 'it looks as if you two have a lot to sort out. Maybe I should let you go wandering around Sydney alone. It's a magical place down there on the harbour, especially at dusk when the lights are coming on.'

'I don't want time alone with Joshua!' exclaimed Leanne at once. 'I planned this weekend to get away from him. I didn't invite him to come with me—he invited himself.'

'A man who knows what he wants and goes all out to get it,' said Cindy. 'I can't fault him for that.' And she glanced at him admiringly.

You don't know him as well as I do, thought Leanne, or you'd never entertain such a notion. She too had once felt that he was perfection personified—until it came to the crunch. And there was no way she was going to change her mind now. If he'd come to Sydney with the intention of trying to win her round he was in for a big disappointment.

'I think,' said Joshua, 'having clearly just dropped a bombshell, I'll go for a swim, if you don't mind, Cindy?'

'Be my guest,' she said expansively.

Leanne breathed a sigh of relief. The tension between them was thick enough to cut with a knife.

'Did you know he felt that way?' asked Cindy as soon as he was out of earshot.

Leanne nodded.

'You could do worse.'

'Don't you start,' she warned her friend. 'I don't love him any more, full stop, end of story.'

Cindy shrugged. 'It's your prerogative. If it were me I'd be falling back into his arms without a second thought. I know what he did to you but it was an instinctive reaction at the time, then pride wouldn't let him back down. Men are big on pride, you know. I think you ought to give him a chance.'

'It wouldn't work; he's hurt me too much. I just don't want anything to do with him. I wish my mother hadn't done this to me.'

'Do you think he'll stay over here even if you don't give him a second chance?'

'I think,' said Leanne quietly, 'that he'll keep battering away at me until I finally give in. Even if it takes years.' She watched as he walked to the edge of the pool. Lord, he looked good. Long, powerfully muscled legs, a flat stomach, a well-developed chest and strong, wide shoulders. There wasn't an ounce of flab on him and he still had the remains of a tan from time spent abroad.

He wore brief black swimming trunks and executed a perfect dive, hardly breaking the surface of the water.

'Some body,' declared Cindy admiringly. 'Bob's developed quite a paunch. I tell him it's all the drinks he has at the golf club. I fancy a swim myself before lunch. What do you say?'

'Not for me,' replied Leanne. 'I'll just sit here— you go and enjoy yourself.'

But watching Joshua was worse than swimming at his side. She couldn't take her eyes off him. Her stomach churned and she felt a need so deep that it frightened her. He and Cindy were laughing and racing each other and suddenly Leanne couldn't stand any more. She rose abruptly to her feet and headed for the house.

'Hey, where are you going?' called Joshua.

She had thought he wouldn't notice and was at a loss for an answer. She couldn't really say that watching him was filling her with a hunger that was scary. It would give him so much ammunition that he would probably come to her room tonight and slake her thirst in a way that only he knew how.

At that moment she heard a sound inside the house. 'I think Bob's just come back,' she said with relief.

She liked Bob. He always treated her like a very dear sister. As soon as she walked in he flung his arms around her. 'How lovely to see you again.'

He was several years older than Cindy and his dark hair was streaked with grey. He had twinkling blue eyes and wore silver-rimmed spectacles, and Cindy was right about him having put on weight.

'What's this?' she asked, patting his tummy.

'Good food on the table and a contented life.'

'That's not what Cindy tells me.'

He smiled. 'So where is that beautiful wife of mine?'

'Swimming with Joshua.'

'Joshua?'

'Yes, the same one,' informed Leanne with a wry smile. 'Cindy was just as surprised. But we're not together again,' she insisted quickly. 'It's a long story; I'll tell you about it some time. Or perhaps Cindy will. I hope you don't mind him staying here. Cindy said it would be all right.'

'If it's fine with my wife then it's OK by me. Why aren't you swimming with them?'

'I feel like being lazy.'

'Then let's get ourselves a couple of drinks and sit and watch them. I have a good bottle of red simply itching to be opened. Not one of yours, unfortunately, but I think you'll like it. And it will give us an appetite for lunch.'

Bob was good company, he made her laugh with some of his tales about antics on the golf course, but sometimes she found herself not listening to him. Instead her mind was occupied with Cindy and Joshua.

Incredibly she was jealous. They were getting on so well, talking quietly together then bursting into peals of laughter. Cindy frequently touched Joshua on the arm or shoulder, something she always did to people—she was a very tactile person—but on this occasion it seemed to Leanne that her friend was deliberately flirting with Joshua, and he was playing up to her for all he was worth.

She could understand him being attracted, but to show it so obviously in front of Cindy's husband was something she couldn't understand. Not that it seemed to bother Bob. He was busy getting down his bottle of red and was quite happy sitting talking.

Deliberately she kept turning her head away but like a magnet it was always drawn back. It wasn't jealousy because she resented the attention he was paying Cindy, she assured herself. There was nothing to worry about there; Cindy was madly in love with her husband and would never two-time him.

She was simply jealous of how well they were getting on. It was how she and Joshua had used to be—*how they could be again,* her conscience assured her, *if only she would forget and forgive. Well, perhaps not forget, you will never do that, but surely you can forgive him?*

But always at the back of her mind would be the fear that it could happen all over again. She dared not let herself get into that situation. Maybe she ought to take Ivan up on his offer and marry him. It would put Joshua safely out of the running. He might even return to England.

'Where are you?' Bob's voice interrupted her reverie.

'I'm sorry. Did you say something?'

'You've not been able to take your eyes off Joshua. It's been a long time since your divorce—almost five years, surely? Is there a chance you'll get back together?'

'Never!' she replied fiercely, but even so her eyes were drawn back again to the man who had both taken her to the heights and then tossed her down into hell.

'Never is a long time, Leanne,' Bob said quietly and kindly. 'Circumstances change, feelings change. The fact that he's here with you now must surely tell you something?'

'He wants me back,' she admitted.

'And would that be such a bad thing?'

'I'm afraid,' she whispered.

'That it might happen again? I wouldn't think so. If he has any sense he'll have learned his lesson.'

'How would you feel if someone told you Cindy was seeing another man? Would you believe them, even if she denied it herself? Would you end your marriage?'

'Actually I think I'd believe Cindy,' he admitted with a wry grimace. 'But all men react differently. And the fact that he wants you back surely means that he's come to his senses at last?'

'No, he hasn't, that's the trouble. His brother told him the truth. And he believed his brother—again. If Mark had said nothing he wouldn't be here now. He'd still be of the opinion that I'd been to bed with him.'

'You don't know that,' said Bob gently. 'He may have spent all these years in purgatory. I know I would if I still loved the woman.'

'So why didn't he come to me? Why didn't he suggest we talk? All he did was divorce me. We've had no contact whatsoever until now. And he's only over here because of his father dying.'

'Yes, Cindy told me. Your mother too.' He put his hand over hers. 'Tragic, very tragic. I feel for you. But life has to go on, as they say. And it looks to me as though Joshua could be the very person to help you.'

They were such a dear couple, both wanting the best for her, but neither of them appreciating the true depth of her feelings. She finished her glass of wine and Bob poured her another, even though she didn't really want it. 'It will do you good,' he insisted.

And shortly after that Cindy and Joshua joined them.

'This is Bob, my husband,' introduced Cindy. 'Bob, this is Joshua, Leanne's—'

'Yes, I know who he is,' interjected the older man. 'How are you enjoying your time in Australia?'

Joshua held out his hand. 'Good, thank you, and many thanks for letting me stay in your home.'

Cindy dropped onto one of the poolside chairs. 'Bob doesn't like swimming much so it was a real treat for me to have company. You should have joined us, Leanne.'

Leanne's eyes were drawn once again to her ex-husband's body. He stood there, tall and proud and savagely handsome as he looked down at her, and for a fraction of time they were alone. She was aware of no one but him. Their eyes met and held and it was almost as though he knew what thoughts were going round in her mind.

An unspoken message zinged between them. Later, he promised, and she agreed, and it wasn't until he'd left them to shower and get dressed that she was able to breathe easily.

She looked at Cindy and Bob to find them both watching her, but nothing was said, and as soon as Joshua returned Cindy announced that it was almost time for lunch. 'Give me a second to make myself decent.'

Joshua and Bob started a conversation about golf, about which she knew nothing, so she sat quietly, engaging in what seemed to be her favourite pastime at the moment, watching Joshua.

His silent promise of spending time together later excited her beyond measure because no matter how much she tried to cut this side of their relationship out of her thoughts, it didn't happen. Her body had a mind of its own and it needed Joshua right at this moment.

When Cindy called them in for lunch she was faintly regretful. She had enjoyed her thoughts, she had enjoyed the heightened feelings chasing around inside her, and was already looking forward to tonight. She was hoping they would spend it together— unless she had read him wrongly. What then? Would she go to him? Her heart raced erratically at the very thought.

Joshua caught her hand as they walked indoors. 'Careful,' he warned in a voice too low for Bob to hear. 'If you carry on looking at me like that I won't be able to wait.'

'I've no idea what you're talking about,' she whispered fiercely.

'Oh, I think you have, and I think that you're as eager as I am. But politeness prevails. We don't want our hosts to feel uncomfortable, do we? But I promise you, Leanne, I won't be able to leave you alone tonight.'

'Nor do I want you to,' she answered, much to her horror. Where had that come from? She certainly hadn't intended to say it.

His smile, faintly crooked as always, was deeply satisfied, and as he squeezed her hand his deep blue eyes sent unnerving messages to her brain. Was this the beginning of her capitulation? she wondered. Was her strength failing? Was she unable to fight him any longer?

'Come on, you two,' Cindy called. And the moment was broken.

Joshua found it difficult to concentrate on eating even though king prawns were one of his favourites, and the Caesar salad one of the best he'd ever tasted. Cindy had placed him opposite Leanne and he couldn't take his eyes off her. The fact that she had agreed to share his bed tonight after the way she had given him the cold shoulder aroused a trillion shivers of salivating anticipation. He felt sure that their hosts must see the electric heat that shot back and forth between them.

But there were still several hours to go before then and, although he was looking forward to seeing some of the city, he knew none of it would match up to the pleasures that lay in store.

The harbour was as spectacular as Cindy had promised. They spent the whole afternoon exploring its surrounds and then didn't see everything. He wanted to climb the bridge but the queues were phenomenal so he contented himself with views from the top of Sydney Tower. The harbour bridge, the opera house, parks and beaches and mountains, he saw them all from their lofty outlook. And then, still in the tower, they went on a virtual adventure tour through Australia's cultural history and geography which he found truly fascinating.

When they returned to the house his mind was spinning with everything new that he had seen, but never once had he lost track of his promise to Leanne. She had done her best to avoid him by trailing along beside Cindy, but he knew that it was because she didn't want her friend to see the sparks that flew hotly between them.

Dinner was booked at a local restaurant and it seemed as though the day would never end. Tomorrow Bob had promised to take them out on his boat so there would be little time for intimacies then. Tonight was his only chance.

It was late when they got back and even then Bob insisted they stay up for a nightcap. Joshua's frustration was running deep and each time he looked at Leanne his male hormones surged to a higher level. Leanne, on the other hand, looked as though she could barely keep her eyes open. He saw his dream of a night filled with passion slowly slipping away from him.

'Poor Leanne,' he said, 'she looks ready to drop. I think it's time we turned in.'

'We should go to bed too,' agreed Cindy. 'Come on, Bob, finish your drink.'

'I'll be up later,' he said, and she rolled her eyes.

While Cindy cleared away their glasses he and Leanne said their goodnights and slipped upstairs. Outside her door Leanne turned to him. 'I'm really tired, Josh. Too much wine, I think.'

He slid his arms around her. 'I have a sure-fire way of ensuring you stay awake.'

'No!' She shook her head. 'It's not on the agenda. I know what I said earlier but I've had time to think and making love with you is not what I want.'

Here we go again, he thought. Mind over matter.

Head over heart. Why couldn't she let herself go for once? He lowered his head and began to nibble her ear lobe—it was the one thing he knew that was guaranteed to arouse her.

'Stop it!' she protested, trying to wriggle free.

But Joshua wasn't prepared to give in. 'I want you, Leanne; you've no idea how much,' he growled, holding her firm. 'I've been waiting for this moment all day. And you can't deny that you weren't ready either.'

'No, I can't,' she said resignedly, 'but it doesn't make it right, and I really am tired, Josh.'

'Then let's simply sleep together; nothing more, I promise.' It was the most difficult promise he'd ever made, but he meant it. Except that he had high hopes that Leanne wouldn't be able to ignore him once they were lying side by side.

'Joshua, no!' she repeated, and, taking advantage of his slackened arms, she pushed open her door and ran quickly inside.

With a slam it was shut and Joshua was left staring at the white woodwork. Disappointment choked him.

Leanne leaned back against the door, her heart banging, her breathing thick and fast. Why had she done that when every fibre of her being craved him? She was a fool to herself. Yes, she had felt tired when sitting downstairs but now she was wide awake and would probably spend the whole night tossing and turning.

Which could easily be cured—by letting Joshua make love to her!

Exactly why had she refused him when she had

been so eager earlier? It was not a question she could answer easily. Fear was the biggest reason. Fear that she would like it too much and be unable to do without it. Fear that she would capitulate and agree to remarry him. Fear that she could be hurt all over again. Or was she being unfair on Joshua? He must have learned his lesson or he wouldn't be here now. He was probably hurting inside just as much as she was. And yet something still stopped her.

She moved across the room and looked out the window at the harbour below. It was quite beautiful with the Technicolor display of lights on the buildings reflecting gently in the waters below, and yet she wasn't able to fully appreciate its splendour because of her disquieting thoughts.

And then came a knock on her door.

'Go away,' she yelled. 'I'm not going to change my mind.'

'Leanne, it's me,' called Cindy.

Immediately Leanne opened the door. 'I'm sorry, I thought—'

'No matter,' said Cindy at once. 'There's a call for you.' And she handed her the telephone.

Leanne frowned. 'Who is it?' she asked, her hand over the mouthpiece. Who could possibly be ringing her at this time of night? Who would know she was here?

'Molly Davis.'

Alarm leapt. Courtney! Something had happened to her. 'Molly, what is it?' she asked at once in a panicky voice.

'Nothing serious,' her neighbour told her quickly. 'Courtney had a fall and she's broken her arm. She's back home now but she keeps asking for you. I don't know whether you can get an earlier flight.'

'Poor darling,' said Leanne at once. 'I'll see what I can do. Is she awake? Can I speak to her?'

'She fell asleep a few minutes ago. Actually I think she only wants to show off her plaster-cast but—'

'It doesn't matter,' said Leanne at once. 'Tell her I'll be there as soon as I can.'

Cindy was still hovering. 'What's happened?'

'My little sister's broken her arm. I must go to her. I hate messing you about but—'

'Nonsense! I'm sorry it's happened. I'll ask Bob to phone the airport, see what he can do.' And she hurried back downstairs.

Leanne banged on Joshua's door and when he didn't answer she walked in. The room was empty but she could hear the shower running. Without even stopping to think she opened the bathroom door. 'Joshua!' she called urgently.

The shower door opened and he stepped out of it, a smile and a look of delighted expectancy on his face. 'I was hoping you'd change your mind.'

'I haven't,' she retorted. 'It's Courtney—she needs me. I must go home.'

'Why? What's wrong?' he asked, plucking a towel from a ready pile and wrapping it sarong-style around his waist.

'Nothing too serious—she's broken her arm—but to her it's the end of the world. I shouldn't have left her; it was far too soon. I was thinking only of myself, and—'

'Leanne, Leanne, don't castigate yourself. These things happen. I'll see what I can do, shall I?'

'Bob's taking care of it.'

'Bob? Is he in any fit state?'

'Maybe not,' agreed Leanne, 'but if he can change our flight then I'll have nothing to complain about. I'm going to pack just in case. I'll never sleep now.'

Bob managed to get them on a flight at nine the following morning but the hours spent waiting seemed interminable to Leanne. They all four sat up drinking coffee and talking desultorily, and Leanne was relieved when the time came for them to leave.

On the plane Joshua placed his hand over hers. 'Don't worry so much. Didn't you ever break a limb as a child? It's something to boast about, not fret.'

'Yes, but she's so young,' protested Leanne.

'And resilient. Don't forget that.'

'I suppose you're right,' she agreed reluctantly.

'I was wondering what Cindy would have thought if she'd found us in bed together.' His smile told her that he found the idea extremely amusing.

'Thank God we weren't,' she returned shortly. How could he think of something like that when Courtney was in trouble?

'Would it have bothered you?'

'It would have been embarrassing,' she admitted. 'On the other hand Cindy thinks we should get back together so she wouldn't have cared.'

'But just imagine if we'd been in full flow.' His grin widened. 'I can't think of anything worse than being interrupted at that precise moment.'

'And is that really all that concerns you?' she rasped. 'Don't you care about Courtney? She's your sister as well, you know.'

'But it's not a life or death situation. Can't you see the funny side?'

'Where you're concerned, no,' she declared flatly. 'I'm thankful that I didn't succumb. And I'm also thankful that this weekend's been brought to a quick end because spending so much time with you is certainly not my idea of paradise. In fact I'm looking forward to seeing Ivan again. There are no complications where he's concerned. I'm seriously thinking about marrying him.'

CHAPTER ELEVEN

'COURTNEY, sweetheart, what have you been doing to yourself?' Leanne hugged her little sister as she came running out of the house, her plastered arm held proudly aloft.

'I falled off a chair.'

'And how did you do that? Weren't you being a good girl for Molly?'

'I dropped my fork. I tried to get it.'

'And fell straight on her arm instead,' informed her neighbour. 'I'm so sorry, Leanne. I should have taken better care.'

Leanne smiled reassuringly. 'Don't blame yourself, Molly. I did much the same thing when I was about seven, though I was climbing a tree.'

'Look, Josh,' said Courtney, and lifted her arm again for his inspection.

Joshua squatted down to her height and looked suitably concerned. 'Does it hurt?'

'No,' said Courtney proudly. 'I'm a big girl.'

'You sure are, honey.'

'I missed you.'

'I missed you, too. And Leanne did. But we're back to stay now so don't ever do anything like that again. Promise?'

'I promise,' said Courtney obediently.

He was so good with her, thought Leanne. If they'd remained married they would probably have had children of their own. One at least, maybe two. Now, if she did have any, it wouldn't be with Joshua. Definitely not.

She had been serious when she declared that she was thinking of marrying Ivan. It felt like the only way out of her present situation. And it wouldn't be all bad because Joshua would go back to England, she had no doubt about that, and with him and his constant temptation out of the way Ivan would be the real friend he'd always been.

They had got on well in the past and her parents had approved of their friendship, so what was wrong with marrying a guy like that?

Someone you don't love? asked her conscience.

I do love him, she protested, in a different sort of way.

And will you be happy with him, or will you keep comparing him to Joshua?

With Joshua out of the way there will be no reason to compare him.

That's wishful thinking.

But that's the way things are going to be, so stop tormenting me.

It's your life.

And that was how she had to look at it.

'Right,' she said to Courtney now, 'let's get you home. And Molly, thank you so much for looking after her. Will you be able to come tomorrow as usual?'

'If you feel you can trust me,' said the older woman wryly.

'Please, don't worry any more about it,' she said,

giving Molly a big hug. 'There's no one I'd rather look after Courtney than you.'

They spent the rest of the day playing with Courtney and it wasn't until the child was in bed that Joshua brought up the subject of Ivan again.

'Were you really serious about marrying Ivan?' They were sitting in their usual spot on the veranda. The sun had gone down, some of the heat had gone out of the day, and darkness was fast approaching.

Leanne had been expecting an interrogation.

'Perfectly serious,' she retorted. 'Before you came here I'd already decided to marry him.' She felt it was a perfectly excusable white lie.

'So why did you change your mind?' he asked, a frown dragging his dark brows together.

'I have no wish to discuss my personal life,' she declared, shaking her head.

'Then I'll tell you why,' he said fiercely. 'It's because you know that life with Ivan will be mediocre. There'll be no excitement, Leanne. I bet you don't even light up inside when he touches you.'

'I didn't know that was a prerequisite of marriage,' she responded tartly.

'It most certainly is,' he said. 'Feel it now.' He placed his hand on her arm and gently stroked and Leanne felt a flare of sensation. This was madness. This was impossible. She wasn't here to be tortured.

She jumped to her feet and glared down at him. 'I'm not standing for this. It's none of your damn business what I do with my life, and the sooner you learn that the better. I'm going to watch TV and I don't want you joining me.'

'You're not running away,' he told her curtly as he

grabbed hold of her wrist. 'It solves nothing. We need to talk about your feelings. We need to find out why—'

'Why I don't want you here?' she finished angrily. 'It's simple. I don't love you.' And that was the truth. She had been in danger of letting her hormones take over. He tormented her body, he tantalised and teased, he made her feel wanton, but that wasn't what she wanted. She wanted to be in a stable relationship, she wanted security, and if that meant marrying Ivan then that was what she would do. Joshua certainly couldn't offer her security. She had painful proof of that.

'I don't believe you,' he said grimly. 'You're fighting it and I know I'm to blame. But if you'd let me I could prove to you that I'll never hurt you again.'

'And how would you do that?' she tossed scornfully. 'Making love won't prove it. Fun while it lasts, yes, but how about the forever? I'm tired of your constant assurances that all will be well if only I'd let myself learn to love you again. You can't say that. You don't know what's around the corner. I've seen a side to you that I don't like, Josh, and I don't want to see it again.'

'You won't,' he assured her, taking both her hands and pulling her close to him. Not quite touching, but near enough to ignite sparks.

'Don't do this,' she groaned, snatching away.

'Do what?' he asked, innocence in his blue eyes, even though she knew that he was perfectly well aware of the feelings he was arousing.

'Blackmail me.'

He gave one of his crooked smiles, the sort that twisted heartstrings, the sort that had had many girls swooning in the past. The sort that could quite easily have her capitulating. But she had to be strong. And what better way to head him off than keep ramming Ivan down his throat? She ought to have carried it on right from the beginning; he might have gone home then and there would have been none of these problems. She had brought it on herself by letting him see that he had the power to get through to her physically.

'There's absolutely no point in us continuing this conversation,' she declared, shooting daggers of resentment from her vivid green eyes. Her whole body was uptight. Persistence had to be Joshua's middle name.

'Because?'

'Because it will get you nowhere. We've been over this so many times it's beginning to bore me. What do I have to say to convince you that you're wasting your time?'

'There is nothing you can say,' he announced, 'because I simply wouldn't believe you. You're forgetting how well I know you, Leanne.'

'Maybe you do,' she riposted, 'but I unfortunately discovered that I didn't know you. And now that I do I want you out of my life.' She was virtually hopping from foot to foot in her distress. She wanted to run away but knew that he would stop her. And she didn't want him touching her because, well, because… Already her heart raced at a thousand beats a minute. Couldn't he see that this whole conversation was pointless?

He folded his arms across his chest and with his head tilted to one side he studied her intently. It was the way he had looked at her when they first met. A considering sort of look, weighing her up, trying to find out what type of girl she was. And he was weighing her up again now, wondering how far he could push her. 'If I thought you really meant that, Leanne, I would be on the next flight back to London.'

'I do mean it,' she reiterated loudly and firmly, her lovely eyes wide and determined on his.

'No, you don't.' He shook his head briefly and that impossible smile still prevailed. 'Not until you have Ivan's ring on your finger will I believe you. And I'm not talking about engagement rings here; that's too simple a solution. Once you're well and truly married I'll back off, but not a second before. Now, let's talk about the winery. I think that—'

'Damn you!' she flung back. 'You're not interested in the winery. It's a diversionary tactic; I should have realised that from the beginning.' She slapped her palms to the sides of her head and rocked it in despair. 'I tell you what,' she said suddenly, 'I'll take out a loan and buy your half from you. Or you can buy my half and I'll skip to the other side of the country. Anything to get you out of my hair.'

'Good try, Leanne,' he said with a grin. 'But it won't work. I'll even let you go now if you give me a kiss.'

Pulses instantly leapt into life—in fact, her whole body surged as though a powerful electric current had arced through it. She knew where that one kiss would lead. She had to make a stand, and do it now, quickly. But it was as though he had read her thoughts and before she could spin away he pulled her against him. She felt the alarming hardness of his arousal and knew with a sense of dread that she had once again lost the battle.

'My beautiful Leanne.' One hand was behind her back, the other cupping her chin. 'I am never going to let you go. You can say what you like but you belong to me, for all time.' And with those ominous words his mouth came down on hers.

Every ounce of fight went out of her, as she had known it would. Capitulation was complete. In a matter of moments she was returning his kiss with a fervour that amazed even herself. Her heartbeats were so fierce that they hurt, and a red-hot heat fired her body.

If he had spoken, if he had said anything at all it would have broken the spell. And he must have known this because he let his actions speak. His kisses devoured, his hands possessed, and fever heat broke out between them.

Quite how they reached Joshua's room Leanne wasn't sure; one second she was on the veranda fully clothed, the next she was lying naked on his bed and Josh was standing over her, shedding his own clothes with indecent haste.

Somewhere in the back of her woolly mind she remembered her wildly abandoned kisses, remembered her fingers digging into the back of Joshua's head as she held him fast against her mouth. And she vaguely remembered Josh groaning, his response becoming more intense, more demanding, until finally he gathered her up in his arms and marched indoors.

And now he was about to culminate those desires. She wasn't quick enough to escape, nor did she want to. Despite her earlier declarations he had worked his magic on her once again and she was his to do with as he liked.

His eyes said it all as he towered over her, two smouldering electric-blue points of light revealing a hunger that went as deep as her own, maybe even deeper. There was an urgency about him that was different.

It would be quick—there would be no preliminaries, none of the foreplay they had so often enjoyed in the past. It would be swift and exciting—and she couldn't wait.

She wrapped her legs around him, pulled him down to her level and kissed him hard. 'Make love to me,' she urged against his mouth. 'Do it *now*.' And she moved her body in a sensual rhythm against his.

He needed no second bidding. She gasped and clung to him, the air draining out of her lungs, finally crying out as spasm after spasm screamed through her body. Seconds later Joshua came to his own body-shaking crescendo.

Slowly he slid off her and they lay side by side, battling for breath, their sweat-slicked bodies shimmering in the dim light that filtered through the window from the veranda.

She felt so vibrantly alive, so deliciously satisfied. It had always been this way with Joshua. He played her with the finesse of a fine violinist. He knew where each of her erogenous zones were and could have her melting to his will in the shortest of moments.

Suddenly she gave a tiny cry and rolled away.

'Leanne, what is it?' Instant concern filled Joshua's voice and he propped himself up on one elbow.

She didn't answer as the awful thought continued

to assault her mind. With an anguished cry she leapt from the bed. But the reality was that it could already be too late.

Joshua wished Leanne would tell him what was wrong. Every ounce of colour had drained from her face and she was shaking as she struggled into the dress he had torn off only a few minutes earlier. He'd had such high hopes. He had actually begun to believe that things were finally going his way, and been looking forward to spending the night together.

He had wanted to make love to her again, but very slowly this time. He wanted to savour every inch of her body, explore in delicious detail every exciting curve and orifice. Now it looked as though it had all been whipped away from him. Once more she'd had second thoughts. And there could be only one reason.

Ivan!

She probably felt that she'd betrayed him and was wondering how she could make love so wildly with one man while planning to marry another. And would Ivan want her if he ever found out? Perhaps this was her torment.

'It's Ivan, isn't it?' he asked bluntly.

'What?' Her eyes glazed over as she looked at him.

'You feel guilty because of Ivan?'

'I shouldn't have let it happen,' she declared in anguish. 'I've ruined my life.'

'No, you haven't,' he assured her. 'All you have to do is marry me instead. Would that be such a hard thing?' He didn't even wait for her answer. 'You know it wouldn't, not after your performance. You were all and more than I remembered, my darling. It would be truly wrong to marry another man, feeling as you do about me.'

By this time he had flung himself off the bed and dragged on his clothes too. And now he took her by the shoulders and forced her to face him. He saw the deep anguish in her eyes and it reminded him of the day he had accused her of having an affair with his brother. He had done it to her again.

Damn! *Damn!* How had this happened? Where had he gone wrong? All he'd wanted to show her was the fatality of marrying a man she didn't love.

'It's not Ivan,' she whispered huskily.

Joshua frowned. Not Ivan! Then what? He was lost.

'Don't you realise I could be pregnant? We didn't take any precautions—we never have. I can't believe I've been so stupid.'

Joshua wanted to laugh but knew that he dared not. 'And that would trouble you?'

'Of course; what do you think?' she snapped. 'Having your baby is the last thing I want.'

That hurt but he tried not to show it. 'I think,' he said, choosing his words with care, 'that it might not even be a possibility. But in any case, would it be such a bad thing, marrying me for the sake of our child? Naturally I'd like you to marry me for a very different reason, but—'

'It would kill me,' she swore vehemently.

'You can't possibly mean that, Leanne.' He heard the hard tone in his voice but could do nothing about it. She was being ridiculous. And he felt the hard glare in his eyes. 'We've just proved how compatible we still are. What else does it take to make you see sense?'

'Love!' she spat.

'I love you.'

'So you say,' she scorned, 'but I don't love you, nor will I ever love you again.'

'Then what are you suggesting, that you'll have a termination if you should be pregnant?' Over his dead body!

She shook her head so fiercely that her hair swung across her face and she looked at him through a honey-blonde curtain. 'I couldn't do that.'

'Then you have no choice.' And he hoped desperately that she was expecting his baby.

'We'll see,' Leanne muttered as she left the room, banging the door loudly behind her. She slammed her own door shut too and he heard her stomping across the floor and the faint creak of her bed as she threw herself down on it. And then there was silence.

He couldn't help smiling. It looked as though the gods were on his side for once. He hadn't deliberately set out to make her pregnant; it had been a heat-of-the-moment thing, on both their parts, and neither of them had given any thought to contraception.

If she did have his baby, and he realised it was a very big if, he would insist that she marry him, even if he had to threaten to take the child off her. Marriage would work between them, he was sure of that. He admired her for sticking to her guns, but deep down inside her there still lived the old Leanne, the one who had loved him unconditionally. And even if he couldn't release her from her tightly locked dungeon, he had every faith that a sweet-smelling bundle of joy would.

He hummed to himself as he got ready for bed. Although their weekend in Sydney hadn't gone entirely to plan it had ended on a high note as far as he was concerned. A very promising high note.

CHAPTER TWELVE

LEANNE was in a quandary. She ought not to have let Joshua see how disturbed she was at the possibility she might be pregnant, because now she would be unable to insist that she was going to marry Ivan. It would even be grossly unfair to date him.

Sleep wouldn't come. Those incredible feelings during the aftermath of lovemaking, which during their marriage she had always savoured to the full, had gone. She was left with nothing but stone-cold dread.

Three times she had let him make love to her, and three times she hadn't thought about the consequences. The faint thought hovered that Joshua might have done it deliberately but she dashed it away. He wasn't that devious. Was he? Surely he wouldn't resort to underhand methods to win her back?

The Joshua she had loved and married would never have done anything like that, but he had turned into a Jekyll and Hyde character. So was his darker side capable of such duplicity? She didn't want to think so, but who knew what the truth was?

Would it be as well to purchase a pregnancy-testing kit and find out once and for all, or dared she wait and see what course nature took? In the end she decided to wait. What difference would it make? It was a matter of ten days, that was all.

Ten days of hell!

She would throw herself into her work. The programme was coming on but it was a long way from being finished. With Joshua out of the house she could get on with it without him intruding into her thoughts.

But it didn't work like that. The image of Joshua wouldn't go away, and when Ivan came to see her she welcomed him warmly. He was the very diversion she needed. She filled a jug of her favourite home-made lemonade and they sat in the cool of the house. There was a real fear of bush fires if the hot weather went on for much longer.

Leanne remembered how they'd spread across the valley some years ago, devastating many thousands of acres of vines. The big-name wineries had survived but some of the smaller ones had been forced to close down. Although she knew that vines regenerated themselves, with a whole year's crop destroyed it had been hard going for some, and if the fire had spread to their vineyard Hugh Lindsay Wines would have been no more either.

'I hear you had to cut short your weekend?'

Leanne nodded. 'Courtney's happy now we're home.'

'Joshua seems happy this morning as well. Is there any particular reason? A likelihood of you two getting back together, for instance?' His blue eyes were troubled as he asked the question.

'You know we're not.'

'I know what you told me, but there has to be something that's put the smile on his face.'

Because he thought he held the whip hand over her, that was why, thought Leanne. He'd probably got everything crossed. 'There's nothing I can think of,' she answered sharply. 'Let's not talk about Josh. What sort of a weekend did you have?'

He lifted an eyebrow and gave her a curious look but he didn't press the subject. He stayed for over an hour and they chatted about anything and everything, and he went away a happier man now that he knew Joshua still wasn't in the running.

But Leanne felt terribly guilty. She had sat there stressing that Joshua meant nothing to her yet less than twelve hours ago she had been in his bed; she might even be carrying his baby. She wondered how she had had the temerity to even face Ivan. He was such a good man and would be dreadfully hurt if he ever found out—which he would if her worst nightmare came true. She would never be able to face him again.

She found it impossible to work after that and spent her time playing with Courtney instead, much to her sister's delight. When Joshua came home at lunchtime she didn't want to face him and told Molly to tell him that she had a headache and was lying down.

But it didn't work because he came to her room and he looked so concerned that she almost weakened. 'Are you all right, Leanne?' he asked quietly, leaning over the bed, where she lay fully dressed.

'What do you think?' she snapped.

'Molly says you have a headache. Have you taken anything for it?'

'I don't have a headache,' she told him dully. 'It was an excuse to keep away from you. Are you too dumb to see that?'

His lips thinned but his voice was gentle as he sat

down on the edge of the bed and touched his hand to her shoulder. 'It was never my intention to do anything that would make you unhappy. You can't blame me; it was a two-way thing. In any case, would it be so awful if you were—?'

'Shut up,' she shrilled, knocking his hand away. 'I don't want to talk about it.'

'Even though it could be a possibility?'

'We'll talk about it when and if it ever happens. Meanwhile just keep away from me.'

'I think we might find that impossible,' he declared, 'since we live in the same house.' And there was a distinct edge to his voice as he added, 'Have you told Ivan?'

'Why would I do that?'

'He came to see you, and he gave me some very strange looks. If you think you can palm this baby off as his then—'

'Shut up, Joshua! As if I'd do something like that! With a bit of luck there won't be a baby.' And if there wasn't—then she'd do everything in her power to get rid of Joshua.

'So why did he come here?'

'Because we're friends, and because he discusses the business with me,' she answered sharply, fed up of his persistent questions.

'And did he do that, discuss the business?'

'Not exactly, not today.'

'So what did you talk about?'

Leanne was fast losing her patience. 'What is this? Why do you always get uptight where Ivan's concerned?'

'Because I don't trust the man.'

'Then get away from here,' she told him loudly, jumping up from the bed and crossing the room, 'because he's a fixture whether you like it or not. My father trusted him, your father trusted him—what the hell's wrong with you? He knows the business inside-out; there's nothing he can't tell you. You really ought to value him. He's the only man here who can tell you everything that's going on. He could run this place single-handed.'

'Then let's hope I'm wrong,' he muttered as he walked out of the room. He didn't even stay for lunch. From the window she saw him marching determinedly back to the winery.

In the days that followed Leanne hardly spoke to him. Joshua did his best to draw her into conversation but she withdrew into herself and always managed to be somewhere else whenever he was around. He worried about her but it seemed that until she found out for sure whether she was pregnant there was nothing he could do.

During their marriage she had been on the Pill because neither of them had wanted to start a family straight away, and he guessed this was the reason he had never thought about contraception. It seemed that every time he felt he was getting closer to her something happened to drive him away again, and he couldn't help wondering whether he was wasting his time.

Maybe, if this proved to be a false alarm, he would be better off returning to England. The thought didn't last long. He couldn't live without Leanne. For five long years he had been in his own private hell. He wasn't going back there. Baby or no baby, he needed her. He had betrayed Leanne once but never again; he loved her too deeply and he had to make her see that.

For the moment, though, he spent more and more time at the winery. He had a good idea now of the various processes and he couldn't wait for Leanne to finish the programme so that he could streamline the office side of things. It was the only thing that bugged him. Even though it was a small business there was no reason why they couldn't be up-to-the-minute in their accounting methods.

And he still thought Ivan was up to something. He'd gone through the books so many times and they didn't add up. Eventually he got his break when he answered the phone late one afternoon. Everyone had gone home, including Ivan, which was unusual because he was always the last to leave, but Joshua had no real reason to rush back these days.

'Ivan, I'm glad I've caught you.' The male voice at the other end didn't wait for confirmation that he was speaking to the right man. 'I'd like another two dozen bottles of Sauvignon Blanc and the same of Riesling. Can you make it tonight? I'll meet you at the usual place.'

Joshua's anger rose swiftly. So that was where the missing wine was going—Ivan was lining his own pockets. But he realised that he needed to keep his calm in order to obtain proof.

'I can't make it tonight, mate,' he said, doing his best to mimic Ivan's voice. It was a talent he had but rarely used, although he had managed to make Leanne laugh on several occasions in the past when he'd taken off various high-profile figures. 'Unless you can come here?'

'But you always said that wasn't wise.'

'Yeah, but I'm on my own.'

'If you're sure,' said the other man uncertainly.

'It's not a problem.'

'OK, I'll be there in twenty minutes.'

Joshua put down the phone and then lifted it again and dialled Ivan's home number. 'Ivan, Josh here,' he said in a hushed, urgent voice. 'I'm still at the winery…I think you should come.'

'Why? What's wrong?' asked Ivan.

'I think we might have an intruder.' Or at least they very soon would have. He wanted to see the two of them together, see their reaction when they realised they'd been found out.

'Have you phoned the police?'

'Not yet. I'm not one hundred per cent sure; I don't want to look silly.'

'Then wait till I come. I'll meet you in the office.'

Joshua grinned as he put down the phone. It would take Ivan less than a quarter of an hour to get here.

He heard the ute long before he saw it, and Ivan cut the engine and let it roll silently down the last few hundred yards before walking silently into the office.

'Is he still here?'

'I'm not sure,' said Joshua. 'All's been quiet these last few minutes.'

'We'd better look around. Where did you hear the noise?'

Joshua didn't want to be away from the office when the other man arrived. It was the only place with a light on, where he would get a good look at this guy who Ivan was supplying with Leanne's wine.

'Wait,' he said, cocking his head. 'What was that?'

They both listened intently and in a matter of seconds a car's headlights turned into the property and a vehicle made its way down to the winery.

'Who can this be?' asked Ivan, moving outside.

Joshua hung back. For the moment he didn't want the other guy to know that there was anyone else present. At the precise moment he stepped out of his car Joshua flicked a switch. The whole area flooded with light.

'Damon!' exclaimed Ivan in panic. 'What are you doing here?'

Damon was short and stocky with jet-black hair and a ruddy complexion. 'You asked me to come.'

Joshua stepped out of the shadows. 'Actually it was I who asked you. I think you have a lot of explaining to do, Ivan. This man wants his *usual* supply of wine.'

Ivan's face blanched. 'I don't know what you're talking about.'

'Oh, yes, you do,' he snarled. 'Damon phoned a little while ago and thought he was talking to you. I know all about your little sideline. What I'm interested in, though, is how many others you supply at Leanne's expense.'

Then he turned blazing eyes on Damon the unfortunate. 'You'd better go before I whip the hide from you. But don't think that this is the last you've heard. I'll be in touch.'

'Who's this guy?' Damon asked Ivan. 'What right has he to tell me what to do?' His fingers were curled into fists and he looked more than capable of standing up for himself.

Ivan shuffled his feet. 'You'd better do as he says; he's one of the owners.'

'The English guy? He didn't sound very English on the phone earlier. He sounded like a true Aussie.'

'Like this, mate?' asked Joshua, slipping easily into Ivan's voice.

Even Ivan looked startled.

Damon didn't say another word; he hurried back to his vehicle, whipping it into reverse and shooting out of the yard as if all the hounds in hell were after him.

'You and I have a lot of talking to do,' Joshua said to Ivan, taking hold of his arm and walking him back to the office. 'Sit!' he ordered peremptorily.

And Ivan sat. He looked scared out of his wits.

'Why?' boomed Joshua. 'And for goodness' sake don't tell me it's a perk of the job.'

'Doesn't every man try to make an extra dollar or two?' Ivan whined.

'Maybe,' agreed Joshua, 'but do they steal to do it? You're on a fair wage. You've even asked the boss to marry you. And yet you do this to her. What will she say, I wonder, when she finds out? My guess is that you'll no longer have a job.'

Ivan winced painfully. 'Do you have to tell Leanne?'

'What do you think?' asked Joshua.

'I'd rather you didn't.'

'Then I'll tell the police instead; let them deal with it,' he announced abruptly. He hadn't time for this man. He had never liked him, and it wasn't altogether due to the fact that Ivan was after his wife. His wife!

Strangely he still thought of Leanne as his wife. Not his ex; never that. His wife. And she would be again, especially after this.

'No!' exclaimed Ivan. 'I'd rather face Leanne than the police.'

'You mean you'll let Leanne call them?'

'She won't do that,' said Ivan confidently.

'I wouldn't be too sure if I were you. Shall we go up to the house now?'

Ivan shook his head. 'I can't face her, not yet.'

Joshua smiled grimly. 'Then I'll tell her for you. In fact it will be a pleasure. But don't be surprised if she gives you your marching orders.'

'Leanne won't get rid of me,' said Ivan with an attempt at bravado. 'She couldn't run the place without me.'

'I'm sure she could with my help,' said Joshua.

'What? You've only been here five minutes.'

'But I have a very retentive brain. I could run things here, have no fear about that. Now you'd better scoot before I change my mind and march you up to the house.'

Ivan needed no second bidding. He looked like a furtive rat as he raced for his ute. Joshua hoped that this was the last he would see of him. Except that he didn't doubt for one moment that Leanne would wish to keep him on. She wouldn't have the heart to sack him. She'd probably feel sorry for him and want to give him a raise.

When he got back to the house all was silent. Courtney was fast asleep and Leanne was nowhere to be seen. She had to be in her room—it was where she usually went when she didn't want to speak to him.

It actually made him feel uncomfortable when she hid away. She shouldn't feel a need to do this in her own house. He tapped on the door, confident it was too early for her to be asleep. And when she didn't answer he pushed it open.

Leanne was curled up in a chair near the window, reading. She wore a cool green T-shirt and a pair of long white shorts, and she looked so devastatingly lovely that his whole body leapt in eager response.

'What do you want?' she asked crossly. 'I thought I told you to keep away from me.'

'How can I do that when you're the most beautiful girl in the world?' he asked gently, moving further into the room and looking down on her. When he inhaled, the delicate perfume of her skin filled his nostrils, making his need of her even greater. Had she no idea how cruel she was being?

It took every ounce of his not inconsiderable self-control to stop him from kissing her. In fact he had to step back a pace. 'But I'm not here to make advances. In fact you don't need to shut yourself away from me, not in your own house. I give you my word that I won't touch you again until you ask.'

'Which will be never,' she slammed.

'So be it.' How he said the words so calmly he didn't know. Never was a long time, he couldn't possibly last that long. 'I'm here to talk business,' he said, his voice suddenly grave. 'There's something you should know.'

Leanne frowned and put down her book. 'Something I'm not going to like, by the sound of your voice. What is it? Wasn't the last harvest as good as we expected?'

'Nothing like that.' He heaved a faintly regretful sigh. 'I'd give the world not to have to tell you this, but it's Ivan.'

'Ivan?' There was deep incredulity in her voice. 'What's Ivan got to do with anything?'

'A whole lot, unfortunately. He's fiddling you.'

'Ivan is? I don't believe you. You've always had it in for him; you're making this up just to discredit him in my eyes.' She jumped to her feet and glared, her eyes the same cool, icy green as her top.

'I wish I were,' he answered sadly.

'So what's he *supposed* to have done?'

'He's taking some of your wine for himself and selling it.'

'And you've seen him do this?' she scorned. 'They all take the odd bottle—it's considered one of the perks of the job.'

'I'm not talking about one or two bottles here, I'm talking dozens,' he answered sharply. 'He has quite a little business going.'

Leanne folded her arms stiffly across her chest and she raised her chin. 'You think Ivan would do that to me? He's my friend; he's been here all his working life. Why would he let me down like that?'

'That's something you'll need to ask him yourself. He's lucky I didn't send for the police.'

'You caught him red-handed? Is that what you're telling me?'

'Precisely.'

'So why didn't you send for me? I could have

sorted it. You probably misread the situation. Maybe he was making a delivery.'

'It was nothing like that, Leanne. Sit down and I'll tell you the whole story.'

'I don't want to sit down!' she yelled. 'You're slandering the man I love. How can I take that sitting down?'

'Dammit, Leanne, this isn't slander, this is fact.' He slammed his hand down on the top of her dressing table and made everything rattle. 'It's about time you lifted your head out of the sand. I took a phone call this evening from one of Ivan's so-called customers. How much more proof do you need than that?'

'So tell me about it,' she snapped.

'He thought I was Ivan. I asked him to come along and collect his order. And as Ivan had gone home I invited him too. If nothing else their faces gave them away. Ivan's supposed to be going to tell you himself, but somehow I can't see him doing it. In fact I'd be surprised if he shows his face here again.'

Leanne shook her head and turned away from him, and when she swung back there was doubt in her eyes. 'I can't believe Ivan would do such a thing. I trusted him implicitly. I can't run the company without him. Are you sure you're not mistaken?'

'I'm not mistaken,' he assured her. 'Why don't you ring him?'

'I will, when I've had time to take it in,' said Leanne, and she sank back into her chair.

'I knew from the stock check that there was wine going missing.' His voice was much quieter now. 'I wanted the computer programme set up so that we could keep a better eye on things. And now I also know why Ivan was so dead set against it,' he added grimly. 'Are you all right, Leanne?'

She was leaning back in her chair, every vestige of colour drained from her face. The shock was too much for her. Especially in her condition! He hadn't thought of that. Of course, they didn't know for sure yet, but he had a gut feeling. 'I'll get you some water,' he said urgently.

He was back from the bathroom in a flash, offering her the glass, standing over her as she drank. 'I shouldn't have sprung it on you like that.'

'It's just that I would never have thought it of Ivan,' she said sadly. 'I'm still hoping it's not true.'

'It's true all right.'

'Should I keep him on, do you think, with a warning? Or get rid of him?'

'I think he'll go of his own free will,' Joshua told her. At least he hoped the man would. He was being selfish, he knew, but with Ivan out of the way he would stand a much better chance with Leanne.

'And if he does go, will we have to bring in another manager, someone who knows the industry as well as Ivan does?'

'There's no need,' Joshua assured her. 'I know enough to keep the company going.'

'Already?' she asked, doubt in her voice.

'Already, my darling. You don't have to worry about a thing.'

Leanne groaned and flopped back in her chair again.

'More water?' he asked solicitously.

'There is such a thing as experience.'

'Of course, but we employ men to do the essential

jobs. They're all good. My skill is in my organising abilities. Hugh Lindsay Wines will run as it never has before.'

'That means you're going to stay in Australia?' she asked weakly.

'You can bet on it,' he answered. 'There'll be no getting rid of me now.'

'In this house?'

'I don't see why not, because if you're having my baby, Leanne, then nothing on earth will separate me from you. And that's a promise.'

CHAPTER THIRTEEN

OVER a week had gone by since the Ivan incident and as Leanne came out of the bathroom she danced and sang in delight.

'Someone's happy this morning,' commented Joshua, emerging from his room at the same time.

'That's because I have something to be happy about.'

'It's not your birthday,' he mused, 'so what could it be, I wonder?'

'I'll tell you,' she sang. 'It's the best news in the world. I'm not pregnant.'

She could see by the sudden flicker in Joshua's eyes that it wasn't good news for him. But as far as she was concerned she couldn't be happier. It had been like a black cloud hanging over her head, that and the fact that Ivan had let her down. But now, all of a sudden, the world had settled back on its axis and she felt good.

Courtney came running along the corridor and Leanne swept her up in her arms, ever heedful of her injury, and whirled to her bedroom. She was grateful for the diversion because she didn't want to talk to Joshua about it yet.

The Ivan affair had cut her up terribly. He had come to see her the morning following Joshua's discovery and she had never seen such a dramatic change in a man. His face had been almost grey and lined with worry.

'It grew out of hand,' he admitted miserably. 'I didn't mean to steal from you, really I didn't. What are you going to do? You're not going to call the police, are you?'

'So it's true?' She still found it difficult to accept that Ivan could do such a thing.

He nodded unhappily.

'I didn't want to believe Joshua,' she said. 'How could you do this to me, Ivan? I respected you; you were my right-hand man. I almost married you. How do you think that makes me feel?'

'No worse than I feel myself,' he said, his head hanging low.

She compressed her lips and shook her head. 'How long's it been going on?'

'Since your father died.'

'You thought my mother and I would be too stupid to notice, is that it?' she questioned, shocked at his revelation. 'Well, perhaps we were, but Joshua isn't stupid.'

'I realise that now; I underestimated him. If you take this no further, Leanne, I'll get out of your life. I'll move away altogether; I'll find another job.'

'I think that might be best,' she agreed.

She felt sad to the bottom of her heart. She had never suspected that Ivan was the type to line his own pockets. It proved she wasn't a very good judge of character.

'Leanne, I'm hungry.'

Snapped back to the present, Leanne finished combing her hair. She had already washed and dressed her sister before getting ready herself. 'Is Molly here yet?'

'Yes.'

'Then let's go and see if she has breakfast ready.'

Downstairs Joshua was waiting for them and Molly hurried in with their breakfast as soon as they were settled.

'You're looking better this morning, Leanne,' her neighbour said.

'I am,' she claimed. 'Much better. And I'm starving.'

Leanne waited until Courtney had finished her breakfast and run away to 'help' Molly, before she asked Joshua the question that was burning at the back of her mind. 'What are you going to do now that you've found out you're not going to be a father?'

He grinned. 'Probably make sure that I do become one.'

Leanne didn't think it was funny and flashed her eyes angrily. 'You know what I mean.'

'You mean you'd like to kick me out?' he asked, his smile fading.

Leanne nodded, even though deep down inside she wasn't entirely sure that this was what she wanted. It would be dreadfully lonely without Joshua, and there would be no Ivan either.

But how could she cope with him living here permanently when there could never be any kind of relationship between them? Nothing had changed. He could ask all he liked and she would never marry him again, so what was the point?

'What if I refuse to go?' His eyes were watchful

on hers, his head tilted to one side, as he read everything that was going on in her mind.

'Then I'll have you evicted,' she declared strongly. 'This house is mine and I don't have to put up with you if I don't want to.'

'Then maybe,' he said with the merest hint of a smile, 'I should persuade you that it would be in your best interests.'

How easily he could do that. Simply sitting here looking at him was enough to almost suffocate her. The heat that sizzled through her body was in danger of setting her on fire.

She pushed herself to her feet and glared down at him. 'Don't you dare lay a finger on me. I suggest you ring a realtor in Tanunda and see what they can offer.' And with that she flounced out of the room.

But she didn't get far. Joshua touched her shoulder and spun her to face him. 'What do I have to say to you, Leanne, to make you see that you mean the whole world to me?'

Where his fingertips touched fire burnt. 'There is nothing you can say,' she retorted. 'Please leave me alone.'

'I thought that with Ivan out of the way you'd—'

'You're glad he turned out to be untrustworthy, aren't you?' she flared.

He grimaced. 'Unfortunately, yes. Not that it seems to have done me much good,' he added bitterly. 'We had more going for us than sex, Leanne; we could capture it again if you'd only melt a little. Is it too much to ask?'

She didn't know how to answer. Yes, it was too much, but at the same time her inner voice kept telling her that she was making a foolish mistake, and if she let him go now she would regret it for the rest of her life.

But how could she be certain of that? 'Go and ring the realtor,' she told him firmly.

For the rest of the day, while Joshua was at work, Leanne tried to concentrate on the programme, which was now nearing completion. Often, though, she found her mind running off at a tangent, mainly in Joshua's direction, and in the end she gave up and went for a swim with Courtney instead.

The water was deliciously cool, the outside temperature baking hot. The dry weather was continuing relentlessly and she was glad they had harvested the grapes.

'Josh! Josh!' called Courtney suddenly, excitedly.

Before she could even turn her head Leanne heard a splash and the next moment he surfaced at her side. Her breath caught in her throat at the sheer male sexuality of him.

'Shouldn't you be at work?' she asked with some irritation. It was bad enough that he intruded into her thoughts without him intruding into her time as well.

'I wanted to see my special girl.'

About to make some smart retort about her not being his girl, she was glad that she hadn't spoken when he lifted Courtney high into the air. Her squeals of delight were a pleasure to hear, and for almost half an hour he played with his little sister while Leanne sat in the shade and watched.

It occurred to her that if she drove Joshua away Courtney was the one who would be hurt the most. She adored her older brother, doted on him in fact, and every night without fail she insisted that he read her a bedtime story. He had taken Steve's place, become a father-figure in fact.

Leanne knew that she was dangerously close to weakening, but still she fought her inner demons. She was afraid that remarrying Joshua wouldn't be the heaven he promised. It would be such a big step to take. How could she possibly know that he would never hurt her again?

She was woken in the middle of the night by Joshua urgently shaking her shoulder. 'Look on the horizon.'

Leanne opened bleary eyes and tried to focus, and when she did she was suddenly wide awake. It was the red glow of fire. They went outside and she could smell the smoke and see the pall that was hanging over the valley.

'Is it coming this way?' he asked.

'Shh!' Leanne was listening intently to the radio she had carried out with her. The news was not good. She turned stricken eyes on Joshua. 'We must be prepared,' she said.

'Shall I wake Courtney?'

'Not yet, but we must pack a bag in case we have to evacuate. Photos, our parents' wedding video, insurance papers, a few clothes. I'll ring Molly, see if she's all right.'

'How about the winery? Is there anything we should save there?'

'Forget it,' declared Leanne hastily. 'It's the house I'm worried about. Get the hose ready in case we need to damp it down.'

She kept an eye on the horizon as she flung things

into a holdall. Molly's son was a firefighter and Molly had told her that he'd been called out several hours ago. 'He said we've nothing to fear unless the wind changes.'

When there was nothing else they could do Leanne and Joshua stood on the veranda and watched and waited.

'I can't do this,' he said at length, 'I have to go and see.'

'What do you mean, see?' she asked in panic. 'There's nothing to see; these fires are dangerous…you could put your own life in danger.'

'Don't worry,' he told her, gripping her arms and looking deep into her eyes. 'If it looks as if it's coming this way I'll be back to get you out of here.'

'You won't have time if there's a fire storm,' she told him worriedly. She could already feel the wind freshening. 'The gases from the eucalyptus combine with the flames,' she informed, 'and depending on the strength of the wind the fire can travel over the tops of the trees at up to two hundred kilometres an hour, sometimes even more.'

'I can't just stand here and wait,' he said quietly. 'I might even be able to save someone's life.'

She wanted to say, I might need you to save my life, but she couldn't. It wouldn't be fair to stop him. She knew he was thinking about his father's death. No one had been able to help him, or her mother.

Her heart thudded as she watched him drive away in his father's four-wheel-drive. And so that she wouldn't stand around panicking she began to fill the bath, as well as all the buckets and bowls she possessed. Hopefully she wouldn't need them, but if there were any flying embers she would be able to douse the spot fires immediately. She had the pool for such emergencies but if the water supply was cut then at least she'd have fresh water.

And while she was doing it Courtney woke up. She was excited to see the fire in the distance and jigged up and down. But Leanne was getting more worried by the minute. She dressed her little sister and even packed her car just in case. Not that she thought there would be a need for quick evacuation, but it gave her something to do.

'Where's Josh?' asked Courtney.

'Gone to help put the fire out.'

'Can me help as well?'

Leanne smiled tenderly. 'I tell you what, let's pretend the house is on fire. We'll turn on the hose and put it out, shall we?'

Courtney nodded enthusiastically. 'Can I really wet the house?'

'Every little bit of it.'

Because of her broken arm, Leanne helped Courtney hold the hose over the veranda, and she was in her element, marching up and down, as they thoroughly soaked everything in sight. Then Leanne took over and aimed it at the walls and as high up on the roof as she could reach. Courtney delighted in running under the spray but Leanne couldn't stop worrying about Joshua.

She didn't fear for herself because she'd lived with the threat of fires all her life, but Joshua didn't know how unpredictable they could be. What if he got too close? What if he got killed? The thought caused her throat to tighten so much that she almost choked. Joshua, dead! She couldn't bear it.

And it was then that the truth hit her. She was still in love with him. She had never fallen out of love. She'd hated him for a while, but not any more. Why hadn't she realised that? Why had it taken a life-or-death situation to bring her to her senses? And what if she lost him now?

Deep, cold dread filled every vein and artery. She turned the hose off and sat down on the veranda steps, heedless of how wet they were. And she dropped her head into her palms.

Two tiny hands shook her. 'Leanne, what's the matter?'

Leanne gathered her sister into her arms. 'I want Josh,' she said.

'Me want him too.'

'Perhaps if we wish hard enough he'll come. Close your eyes, baby, and wish.'

Courtney screwed her eyes shut and Leanne did the same and they both wished as hard as they could. When they opened them again he still wasn't there— but the fire had breasted the hill and was beginning to sweep across the valley.

Leanne could faintly hear the crackle and pop of the stringy bark gums as they burst into flames; she even fancied that she could smell the eucalyptus oil, and the faint shouts of the firefighters were carried on the air towards them. Even though it was beginning to get light, the whole sky was an ominous red and a thick haze of smoke hung everywhere.

When she heard a vehicle approaching she thanked the lord that Joshua had returned, but it wasn't him—

it was a fireman come to warn them to get ready to evacuate.

Whole acres of vines were being destroyed in seconds. Molly phoned to tell her that she was leaving, that another of her sons had come to collect her. 'Come with us,' she said, but Leanne didn't want to leave without Joshua. She was confident he would be back in time.

But he wasn't back, and as the fire drew nearer, as the noise got louder, as Courtney began to cry, Leanne knew that she would have to go. Then a car screamed to a halt in front of the house. But again it wasn't Joshua.

'What are you doing still here?' asked the male voice.

'Ivan!' Leanne felt tears slide down her cheeks. She was trying to be brave for Courtney's sake, but the relief of having someone to help was overwhelming.

'Get in the car,' he ordered.

'I have my own already packed.'

'Then follow me. What the hell are you doing still here?'

'Waiting for Joshua.'

'Where is he?'

'I don't know.' Fresh tears squeezed out of her eyes and rolled down her cheeks. 'He went to—to look at the fire. I know it was stupid but I couldn't stop him. He's probably helping. I'm sure he'll be all right.' Brave words because she wasn't sure—anything could have happened to him.

'He should be here, helping you,' snarled Ivan. 'Let's go.'

And so Leanne made the agonising decision of leaving her home, and leaving without Joshua.

They drove to Ivan's parents' home some fifty kilometres away. 'You'll be safe here,' he said as he prepared to get back into his car and drive away.

'You're not staying?'

'No, you can't possibly want me around after the way I treated you.'

'But—'

'But nothing,' he said swiftly as he slammed his car door. 'Just take care of yourself.' And he was gone.

When Joshua got back to the house and found it empty he was at first relieved that Leanne and Courtney had got away safely, but then came concern because he didn't know where to find them. The fire was so close that he knew he dared not stay here any longer, but where did he go?

What he had seen earlier, the incredible bravery of the firefighters, most of them volunteers, had made him feel very humble. This was nature at its voracious worst. He'd helped people evacuate their homes, he'd seen how quickly the buildings went up in flames, and he'd done all he could, all the time knowing that there had been no one to rescue his father or Pauline. It really had brought home how terrifying it must have been for them.

As he was about to leave a car hurtled into the drive in front of him. Ivan leapt out. 'Thank God you're safe; Leanne's out of her mind with worry. Let's get going, mate—she's at my parents' house.'

There was no time to ask questions, but on the long

drive Joshua's mind was churning. How had Ivan got involved? Leanne must have phoned him; she must have been at her wits' end when he didn't return and she had no one else to turn to. He hadn't realised how quickly the time had gone, nor how close to their vineyard the fire had spread.

Even in the few short minutes he'd been here it had reached their vineyard but the firefighters were hopeful of having it under control. Helicopters overhead had dropped thousands of gallons of water scooped up from a local lake, but he didn't have time to watch because Ivan was urging him away.

Whatever he thought of the man he was grateful to him for helping Leanne. He couldn't believe how incredibly stupid he had been to go off and leave her like that. He simply hadn't realised how greedy and cruel these fires were, how fast they could travel. Even though Leanne had warned him.

But he would make it up to her. He would do all in his power to bring her life back to normal. If they lost everything he would rebuild for her. He would make sure that she wanted for nothing.

When they reached the house Leanne ran out and threw herself into his arms. 'Thank God you're safe, Josh. I've been so worried.'

It was almost worth the trauma of the last hours to hear those words. He held her more tightly than he ever had before. 'Me too, my darling.'

'I thought you were dead.' The words choked out of her. 'I thought I was never going to see you again.'

'There was no chance of that,' he told her thickly. 'I was always going to come back to you. I must admit I was fazed when I found you gone, until Ivan turned up and told me where you were.'

'I was waiting for you. I'd have gone on waiting if he hadn't come and got me. I think it was guilt— he wanted to repair some of the damage he'd caused. I didn't know he was coming back to look for you, though. He's certainly gone up a notch in my estimation.'

'Mine too, if that's what happened,' said Joshua. 'But what matters at this moment is that you're safe. We'll talk about Ivan later. Would you really have put your own life in danger waiting for me?'

Leanne nodded.

It was sounding good. 'Does that mean you do care for me—a little bit?'

'It means,' said Leanne slowly, her lovely green eyes luminous as they looked into his face, 'that I've come to my senses. I still love you, Joshua. I love you very much.'

Joshua felt his heart begin to race. 'Are you serious?' This was so much more than he'd expected.

'Very sure. I should have known it all along; I should have known I could never fall out of love with you.'

'Nor I you, my precious.' He was black from the fire, his clothes stank, but he was sure it didn't matter. He kissed her, a hard, long kiss that took their breath away. 'I always hoped for this moment,' he told her thickly, his mouth grazing hers, 'but I never truly believed it would happen.'

'Neither did I,' she admitted. 'I was determined never to fall in love with you again. We had great sex but I told myself that's all it was. Now I know differently. Sex without love could never be as satisfying.'

'I think,' he said slowly, 'that if I'm to reaffirm your opinion, and I'd very much like to do that, then we should ask these good people if I can use their bathroom.'

'More than that,' she said with a cheeky smile, 'they're letting us stay here until all danger has passed. Is the house still standing?'

'Thankfully, yes. We might lose a few vines, but I think the worst is over. The wind appears to have turned again, thank goodness.'

Leanne felt as though she was walking on air. She was in love with Joshua and he was safe. Nothing else mattered. Ivan's parents had seen the way she greeted him, and probably knew the whole story, because they simply smiled when she told them that Joshua would be sharing her room.

Ivan had disappeared again; he hadn't even stopped once he'd shown Joshua where she was. As far as she was concerned he was the hero of the hour and if he wanted to come back and work for her she would let him. She felt very sure that he'd learned his lesson.

Courtney had been given her own little room and was fast asleep, the excitement of the events taking its toll, and Leanne waited in the bedroom with her heart beating like an urgent jungle drum.

When Joshua strode in, a navy towel around his loins, a whole host of other urgent emotions added to the drum-beat. She expected him to want to make love to her immediately, but instead he sat her down beside him on the edge of the bed.

'Tell me I'm not imagining things,' he said, taking her hands into his. 'Did I hear you say that you loved me, despite everything?'

Leanne nodded.

'And there's no likelihood that you'll change your mind?'

'None at all.'

'You don't love Ivan?'

'I never have—we've not even made love.'

Joshua frowned. 'But I thought—'

'He was mending a hinge,' she cut in with a huge smile.

'So you let me jump to conclusions?' he asked with pretended anger.

'It suited my purpose.'

'You little minx, you really had me going. But I promise you I'll never make any more false accusations.'

'I think we should put the past behind us,' she said, lifting her mouth for his kiss.

With a groan he captured her lips and after that time held no meaning. Their lovemaking was more urgent and more satisfying than it had ever been. They had come through the storm and found themselves again. Nothing or no one would ever part them now.

'Will you marry me?' he asked gruffly as they lay spent on the bed.

'Yes,' whispered Leanne.

'Will you bear my children?'

'Yes.'

'Will you live with me into old age?'

'Yes.'

His satisfied smile said it all.

'Now my turn,' she said. 'Will you live with me here in Australia?'

'Yes.'

'Will you be a good father to our children, Courtney included?'

'Yes.'

'And will you—?'

'Yes to everything,' he declared firmly. 'Now, no more talking—I need to make love to you again, and again, and again…'